A CIRCLE OF DRAGONS & BABIOLA

TWO STORIES BY PRUFROCK

A.J. PRUFROCK

A NOTE FROM THE EDITOR

Dear Reader,

There is no such thing as an original tale, and—if Google is to be believed—in all of literature there is a whopping total of six plots. All an author can do is cull, rearrange, reframe, and refresh, according to his own life experience.

The origins of the about-to-be read stories—if the introduction to Mrs. Valentine's *The Old Old Fairy Tales* is to be believed—are truly international. Mrs. Valentine culled from Hungary, Russia, Serbia, Romania, Sicily, Finland, Iceland, Japan, Portugal, and any country "impacted by the Crusades." Andrew Lang—once again a provider of Prufrock inspiration—claims much the same. We also admit the works are under the heavy influence of Peter Christian Asbjornsen's *East of the Sun and West of the Moon,* a collection of Old Norse folk tales.

Mrs. Valentine concerned herself with editing out all "coarseness unsuitable for children." Mr. Asbjornsen was sure he was "reincarnating the roots of all antiquity." Prufrock has no similar noble goal. In fact, he has put a little coarseness back in and may have snipped an antiquated root or two.

A Circle of Dragons and *Babiola* are both saunters through public-domain fairy tales in search of steal-worthy characters, dialogue, and plot points. Where Lang and Valentine's influence stops and Asbjornsen's starts is hard to tell, even with gutenburg.org available at everyone's fingertips. We suggest you, the reader, sit back and enjoy Prufrock having his most fun.

Sincerely,
    L.E. Gillquist
    Editor Supposedly-in-Charge

A CIRCLE OF DRAGONS

[1]

UNEXPECTED GUESTS

Tell me of the peoples ways
The ends and outs of all their days
Dare they believe that when they die
They soar above where dragons fly?

Hilda Kenterick had been alone in the cabin for a week now. Mother had sent her over a well-known path to join her father and brother in the forest outpost, but Hilda had been greeted only by a note balanced upon the wide mantle above the hearth. Father's scrawl indicated the two would return by morning. Seven mornings had passed.

One early afternoon while Hilda sat enjoying one of Father's favorite books[1], three large shadows passed across the window pane. Her bare feet felt the largeness of whatever had lumbered into the front garden, heavy vibrations radiating through the slatted floor. Hilda's whole body now trembled in sympathetic waves. No one but family knew the cabin's locale and friends never came to call.

In haste, she set the book aside and took stock of the encroachers through a chink in the logs.

Hilda was fortunate. Her parents had set facts plainly before their children. Since she could walk, there had been no coddling nannies and overprotective tutors buffering her from the wildness of the outside world. Though she had never before seen a dragon, she knew a rhyme to help distinguish one species from another—

Green of scale and yellow-eyed
Rekiki, by troll meat is satisfied

Two guests were definitely Rekikis. "Too bad I have not a single slice of troll in the root cellar," Hilda muttered, trying to use humor to choke back her fear. She pulled hard at childhood memories and extracted a second rhyme to identify the third figure—

Sarkani, great in fang and claw
By mere presence kills with awe

But if guest number three was a Sarkani, it was only an adolescent, for the beast was yet to develop the fatal dread its presence was reputed to carry. Still, the look of it caused a shiver to crawl up and down Hilda's spine.

There was a third rhyme for a third kind, but if a Zendino was coming, it had not yet appeared.

Hilda's father and brother had taken the weapons. Even with the remaining well-sharpened kitchen knives, the battle was three against one, gargantuan trio against a little girl. There was no use running. No one outran dragons. They had to lose interest, and these seemed to be growing in their curiosity. There was nothing to do but to invite them to tea.

Hilda burned her father's note, stoked the fire in the wood-burning stove, checked the kettle, and stepped out into the yard.

"Greetings!" she called with feigned naivety. "Can I refresh you on your travels? There is not much in the pantry, but I can put on a pot of tea."

Each visitor turned towards Hilda, then back to each other. They were used to humans cowering, scurrying, and screaming. Hospitality was a fascinating novelty.

One of the Rekiki spoke first, clapping fore-claws together, "Oh how quaint! Let's do! Let's do!"

Her near-twin was quick to answer, "Yes, let's do. Let's have a tea party like the peoples, hosted by a small human." She glanced to both her companions, adding, "I believe this young one is female."[2]

The intruders conferred among themselves, then bowed low to accept the invitation. Hilda pointed to a circle of stumps around a fire pit and invited her guests to rest there. She returned to the cabin, careful to hide her continued shaking. As she went, she heard the Sarkani say, "Perhaps when Geraldine arrives, we can make a campfire and tell stories, like the peoples do."

So a fourth is coming and they don't intend to leave any time soon, thought Hilda, her stomach dropping.

As Hilda found cooking pots to act as teacups, voices filtered in from the yard, "Perhaps the girl—'girl' is what baby humans are called, right?—will teach us the human songs that humans sing while roasting their tiny globs of goat meat over an open fire. What great fun!"

"You and your 'fun,' Jolene," scorned a sour voice. "We are on a mission."

"Fun is fine, Loretta, if done along the way," answered back the chipper voice of Jolene. "We can't do much more than wait until Geraldine joins us again. We might as well learn the ways of peoples while we wait. I hear they don't live long, so let's all do our best not to frighten. The young one shows spirit and might teach us much."

"I am in no mood," grunted Loretta, "and will never be, to take lessons from a human girl."

"You will if it is useful to our quest," hissed the third voice of the Sarkani.

"No one made you boss, Wynona," shot back Loretta in return, "just because Geraldine sent us on ahead."

Hilda emerged with three copper pots and a sugar jar, balanced upon a large wooden tray. Wedged between was a small tin cup holding a spot of tea for herself. Hilda placed the tray upon the cornerstone of the fire pit, handed each guest a steaming beverage, curtsied, and asked, "Cream or sugar?"

By the time the words left Hilda's mouth, Loretta's pot was empty. The others pointed and laughed at her overeagerness. Tea dripped from the corners of the wide reptilian mouth as she fumed.

"You don't get out much, do you?" cackled the caustic tones of Wynona, "Did you get zero education in human custom?"

"If you want more, I can get it for you," offered Hilda.

"No. Don't bother. I was drinking for show. I am not in the least bit thirsty and this stuff is overpraised," Loretta said. She stared at Wynona with a look that made Hilda shudder. Hilda refilled her pot anyway.

"*I'd* like sugar," said Wynona, ignoring Loretta's glare. Wynona reached—all the while trying to smile with politeness through snaggled teeth—to take the entire canister out of Hilda's hands.

Hilda stepped back out of reach, bowed again, and asked with demure firmness, "One lump or two?

It was Loretta's turn to cackle. "Get out much?" came the mocking echo, "What was that about human custom?"

Jolene had stifled laughter twice now, for it was her careful habit to stay out of the volatile in-between of her two companions. "Don't mind our banter," she whispered to the hostess. "We'll all drink it black."

Hilda nodded, and took the canister back inside. When she returned, she took up her tin cup and sat with her visitors round the fire. Each of her guests held her pot with an awkward fist and watched the young human's every motion.

"I could not help but hear a few names bandied about while I brewed your tea," Hilda began. "Which of you is Loretta? I think I also heard the names Jolene and Wynona."

The guests were impressed. To be named and treated like ladies made them forget to be suspicious of Hilda's listening ears.

"I'm Jolene," piped up a Rekiki, "and this is my sister, Loretta. We hatched from the same clutch, two strong ones who survived." Hilda made a rhyme in her head—

Rekiki Loretta
Rekiki Jolene
One seems nice but both are mean

Wynona blinked and added, "So it's obvious who I am." Hilda continued making verse—

Wynona Sarkani
Claws do gleam
Leads in place of Geraldine

Hilda noted that Wynona and Jolene made a game of imitating her, attempting small sips, while Loretta gulped, belched, and shot forth a mocking command, "Human girl, little darling, take my order. I'll have wild boar stuffed with pigeon and in each pigeon, a marinated sparrow."

"Don't tease her," scolded Jolene, "she is a young one I tell you!"

Hilda stood and apologized, "I'm afraid, until the men come back from the hunt ..."

"Men coming! When?" exclaimed Jolene, her voice rising, her head twisting round.

"I don't know. They're gone for weeks sometimes," said Hilda. She noted the rise in Jolene's pitch. "But until they return, I have nothing to offer you but jerky, flat cakes, and oatmeal. There's nothing worthy of guests, I'm afraid."

"Ignore Jolene, little people-girl," said Wynona. "You poor humans, having to eat so constantly ... once a week is often enough for us. Loretta here is still digesting half an ox."

"What a feast," mused Loretta, rubbing her belly.

"And," continued Wynona, "if we were hungry, we would not be sitting round sipping your tea."

Hilda turned white and sat down.

"I am not so ignorant as my comrades, human," Wynona said. "Tell us stories. If they please us, we might let you live. Mind that the tales have dragons in them. You do have stories with dragons, don't you?"

Hilda nodded.

"And people-girl, tell them just as your mother and her mother before her told them. Skip nothing, add nothing. I wish not only to be entertained, but enlightened. Let us, we three dragons, get to know you peoples better."

Jolene and Loretta looked on, unblinking.

Hilda took her last sip of tea, and began.

[2]

THE SECRET DREAM OF TOBIT
QUATTLEBAUM

I had a dream
Till it comes true
I'll tell no one
Especially you

*Tamar Quattlebaum could not keep a husband any better
than she could keep a secret. She did manage to keep—for
a while anyway—a little son she liked to call Tobit (though the
man who sired him called him something else altogether).*

Hilda felt ill at ease. She was used to telling stories but not
used to anyone paying attention. The mesmerized dragons
could not tell. They had not expected this level of sophistica-
tion from one so young. Infidelity and a gossiping tongue in the
first two lines ... fascinating!

*Tobit's one distinction from all the other boys his age was an
obsession with an old scabbard his father had left behind. He
wore it always, though his mother pretended not to notice it
hanging constantly from his belt. Mother Tamar used the same
expert selective memory she employed in pretending the man*

who once owned the sheath never existed to begin with. This was the reason she did not notice that, as Tobit grew, so did the scabbard.

The brows of all three tea-sipping dragons were raised. Hilda did not notice and continued without pause.

The sword which belonged in the empty scabbard was buried to its hilt on the edge of Tamar's property where the apple trees brushed the edges of the vegetable garden. Every year on his birthday, Tobit would go out to see if he were strong enough at last to pull the blade from the ground. He wondered often if the matter of extraction had more to do with the willingness of the sword rather than the size of his muscles. Whatever the reason, he longed for the day he would place the blade into the scabbard hanging from his waist.

Loretta suppressed a snicker and swallowed hard. Hilda focused on the more serious face of Wynona and pressed on.

The year that both sword and sheath were just the right size, Tobit was only going through the motions of trying. He had awakened from the most marvelous dream and was still pondering its mysteries when he stumbled to the garden out of birthday habit. When he gave the customary tug, the weapon slipped from the earth with such ease that the young man found himself flat on his rumpus, holding the great blade up in the sunlight. Tobit was delighted, but determined to not tell anyone about his accomplishment, particularly his mother. He loved her, but accepted the sad fact that she could never keep anything from the neighbors. He put the sword back in the hole and went in to breakfast.

*It is one thing to keep a secret when others do not wish to see, but quite another when they are determined to know. Tobit said nothing outright, but his face did not hide the fact that **something** had happened. Before he had swallowed his first bite of gruel, his mother asked him why he was glowing with pride, like* *one who had unearthed buried treasure. Tobit was troubled how close she had come to a part of the truth, but only answered, "Oh, mother, I had such a nice dream last night!" Then catching himself, he added, "but I can't tell it to anybody."*

"You can tell it to me," Tamar answered. "It must have been a nice dream, or you wouldn't look so happy."

"No, mother. I can't tell it to anybody," said Tobit, "until it comes true."

"For crying out loud, I am your mother!" Tamar cried. "Know the dream, I will!"

But it was no use. Neither threats, nor beatings, nor meals withheld could get the secret out of the boy. There was such strife between mother and son that often Tobit would run out into the garden and collapse weeping. When his fits occurred near the buried sword, the weapon would work itself round and round, whirling in its hole. But the moment Tobit stretched out his hand, it stopped and let him slide it out of the hole and into the scabbard. It was strangely comforting, and strange company to keep.

Hilda looked across the fire at the strange company she herself was keeping. Jolene and Loretta were elbowing each other and shooting sideways glances. Wynona boxed them on their pointy ears and gruffed, "Grow up. She is too young to follow the multiple meanings and you are both too old to be giggling at double entendre. Pay attention and learn!"

Jolene and Loretta sobered. Wynona, with the tone of a schoolmarm, instructed, "Lesson one—old human-nags hate secrets as much as mother dragons do, both to the point of abusing their young."

Hilda had never noted that point in the story, even though she had heard it year after year. She had always hurt too much for Tobit's tears to pay much attention to his mother's frustration.

There was no time to ponder. This was a long tale and it would be some time before dragons entered the story. Hilda would not mind if her guests continued their sniggering and ear-boxing as long as the tale did not grow old to the listening reptilian ears.

DURING ONE OF *his sobbing fits, unbeknownst to Tobit His Highness King Humphrey came riding along. The king heard the sounds of distress and stopped his coach. "Footman!" he ordered, "Go and see who it is that is crying."*

In a few minutes, the servant returned and answered, "It is just a young boy, sire, being disciplined for disobedience."

"Humph!" cried King Humphrey. "Bring him to me at once. I can't stand for a child to cry."

"Yes, my lord," answered the servant, who was very familiar with how this exact weakness in the face of tears affected the king's rearing of his daughters. Keeping his child-rearing opinions to himself, the footman went to Tobit, instructed him to dry his tears, and brought him to the royal carriage.

King Humphrey was at once smitten with the noble-looking youth and exclaimed in a magnanimous tone, "Will you be my son, boy?"

"Certainly, sire," answered Tobit. "If my mother will let me."

King Humphrey called for Mother Tamar and went through the motions of asking permission. He told the greying woman he intended to adopt her boy, adding with a wink that, if he proved worthy, Tobit might even marry a princess one day.

Tamar's resolute anger with Tobit now turned into joy. She began kissing King Humphrey's hand, cooing, "I hope ... kiss-

kiss ... he will be ... smack-smack ... more obedient ... smooch-smooch ... to His Majesty than he has been to me."

This outbreak of distracting affection gave time for Tobit to slip back into the garden and retrieve his beloved sword. Neither the king nor his mother noticed him leave or return. After a bow to his mother, Tobit climbed into the king's coach and blew kisses as he was driven away.

When they had gone some distance from Tobit's home, and the tops of the orchard trees had faded from view, King Humphrey turned to his newly acquired boy and asked, "Why, my dear son, were you crying with such bitterness in the garden?"

"Because my mother had been beating me," said Tobit straightaway.

"And why," questioned His Majesty further, "would a woman wear herself out beating a fine lad like you?"

Tobit answered without hesitation, "Because I would not tell her my dream."

"And why would you not tell it to her?"

"Because I will never tell it to anyone until it comes true," said the boy.

"Humph," said King Humphrey, "I bet you'll tell it to me."

"No sir, not even to you, Your Majesty," said Tobit.

"Oh, I am sure you will when we get home," said the king smiling and spoke no more of the matter while they traveled.

[3]

TOBIT AND MERRIWETHER

Those who tell the truth don't swear
Those who can't convince demand
Those refused might shriek and shrill
And think to master and command
But nose and mouth and foot and hand
And sparkling eye and tongue all know
That outer man aches to display
Integrity of inward soul

That evening, Tobit and the king arrived at the palace. King Humphrey's three daughters ran out to meet the carriage, crying, "What did you bring us, Daddy!?"

The king laughed so hard his belly shook. He presented Tobit to them saying, "I have brought you such a nice present, my angels. A beautiful boy." All three girls were delighted, and though their father admonished them not to spoil Tobit, they fell over each other giving him their best toys.

"Toys for the boy toy," giggled Jolene. Loretta rolled her eyes. Hilda resumed.

The next day King Humphrey went out on his balcony to watch the four children play together on the lawn below. "He has a secret, my daughters!" the king called out, "that he says he will tell no one."

"He will tell me," said the eldest princess, Flora. Tobit shook his head.

"He will tell me," declared the second girl, Fauna. Tobit shook his head.

"He will tell me!" cried the youngest, Merriwether who knew she was the prettiest and most charming.

"I will tell nobody until it comes true," said Tobit to them all, "and it is best not to ask me."

The king was very sorry to hear this for he liked Tobit very much. But he also knew it would never do to keep anyone near him who would not do as he was ordered. Tobit was expelled from the palace that very day and sent to live in the servants' quarters. King Humphrey was sure he would come to his senses when he began to miss the girls and their playthings.

The sword clanked as Tobit was led away from Humphrey's palace, but the boy said nothing. He was saddened by his treatment, but the servants and their children were very kind to him and he soon grew merry again.

Tobit lived with the servants and as a servant until his seventeenth birthday.

THE THREE PRINCESSES grew up into lovely young women. Flora and Fauna married two powerful kings who ruled over great countries across the sea. But Merriwether was particular and turned up her nose at all the young princes who had sought her hand.

One day Merriwether was sitting in the palace feeling so

bored she began to wonder what the servants were doing. Her father was in council discussing the sudden arrival of a Pannonian envoy, and, since her mother was ill in bed, there was no one to stop the princess from running across the gardens to the houses where the help lived.

In the courtyard at the center of a cluster of cottages, Merriwether noticed a youth who was handsomer than any prince who had come to court her. In an instant, she recognized him to be the little boy she had once played with so long ago.

"Hello Tobit," she said, crossing the ground between them.

"Hello, Princess Merriwether," Tobit said with a bow, surprised he could remember even his own name in the presence of one who had grown so beautiful.

Merriwether came close and took both of Tobit's hands into her own. She could feel the young man tremble as she pressed her lips close to his ear and whispered, "Tell me your secret, Tobit, and I will get Papa to let me marry you."

Tobit wrapped Merriwether in his arms, more tightly than the pampered princess was used to. He could feel her tremble as he whispered back, "I will tell nobody until it comes true. And it is best that you not ask me."

With that, Tobit pushed her away and turned on his heel. Merriwether watched him disappear among several pretty servant girls, and felt anger boil in her veins.

"I heard a similar story ..." interjected Loretta, "from the mouth of a princess my uncle tied to a spit. The about-to-be-roasted highness said Tobit beat the girl for her brazenness ..."

Hilda was glad not to be telling stories from a spit.

Wynona squinted and peered at her, "You aren't adding anything, human? Not skipping anything, are you? Cleaning it up for the times? I think I was crystal clear about giving us unedited versions. Oral history should be passed along unchanged ..."

"No, ma'am," answered Hilda. "It may have been changed by someone, but not by me. I'm telling it just as my mother told it. I suppose the about-to-be-roasted princess was stressed and forgot how it went."

"Swear."

"No need, since I do not lie."

"Fair enough. Continue."

Hilda tapped her forehead to find her place, mumbling, "Where was I? ... watched him disappear ... several pretty servant girls ... anger boiling ... ah yes."

Princess Merriwether turned on her heel as well and ran home to complain to her father. She told King Humphrey that, while she was out gathering flowers for her ailing mother, she had been jeered, mocked, and shoved by the wretched servant, Tobit.

"If he had a thousand souls, I would kill them all!" swore King Humphrey.

That very day King Humphrey ordered gallows built outside the palace and invited all his subjects to come to see the execution of a young man who had dared to insult a king's daughter.

The next morning, Tobit was brought out blindfolded with hands tied behind his back. When his sentence was read, he felt the sword clank within the scabbard against his side.

As the guard led Tobit to the noose, a great noise was heard. A golden coach rumbled over the stones, with a white flag waving out of the window.

It stopped underneath the gallows, and from it stepped the ambassador from Pannonia. "King Humphrey, good friend," the stranger in fine clothes called out for all to hear. "Since you have no use for this miscreant, might I have him?"

"Sir," replied King Humphrey, "He has publicly insulted the royal princess and even dared to lay a hand upon her. I cannot pardon that!"

"Send him with me to Pannonia, Your Majesty, and I assure you he will learn manners and great humility."

"Well. Humph," said King Humphrey, who, if he were honest with himself, would have admitted he was of two minds concerning Merriwether's testimony. "If you want him so much you can have him. Only let me never see his face again!"

When the blindfold was removed from Tobit's eyes and the cords from his wrists, he found himself seated in a golden coach beside a royal ambassador on his way to Pannonia.

THE AMBASSADOR WINED and dined Tobit all the way to their destination, and the very hungry young man appreciated both every bite and every sight along the way.

After they had gone some distance, the ambassador leaned in and asked, "Why, my dear son, were you **really** condemned to hanging? How did you stir up the fury of the princess?"

Tobit answered without hesitation, "I would not tell her my dream."

"And why wouldn't you tell it to her?"

"Because I will never tell it to anyone until it comes true," said Tobit.

"Perhaps you will tell it to me ..."

"No sir, not to you, nor even to your king," replied Tobit.

"Oh, I am sure you will when we get home to Pannonia," said the ambassador smiling. He spoke no more of it while they traveled.

The journey to Pannonia was very long. When they arrived, King Wittlesbach's daughter (who was as beautiful as the morning star) happened to be picking roses in the garden. The ambassador was sure, seeing Tobit take in her beauty, that the young man's secret was as good as told.

"Oh, what a handsome youth! Have you brought him from fairyland?" cried Princess Pasha.

"Word has reached me, ambassador," bellowed King Wittlesbach, trying to hide the fact he was vexed at his daughter's open words of admiration, "that you have saved this youth from the gallows."

"I don't care where he is from," said the determined princess. "I will marry him and nobody else."

"He is no better than a recalcitrant servant," said her father, growing ever louder.

"That is nothing to me," said Pasha, "for I love him and to me he will open his heart."

King Wittlesbach shook his head in dismay, and gave orders that the guest was to be lodged in the summerhouse.

$$[\ 4\ ]$$

TOBIT AND PASHA

Love and passion, though different grapes
Make wines that smell and taste near same
One sipped slow, one downed in haste
And bitter dregs to one pertain

One week later to the day, Princess Pasha put on her finest form-fitting dress and went to pay Tobit a visit. She looked so beautiful that at the sight of her a book[1] dropped from his hand and he stood up speechless. "Tell me," she said, coaxingly, "what is this wonderful secret? Just whisper it in my ear, and I will give you a kiss."

"My angel," Tobit said, "Be wise and ask no questions. I have kept my secret all these years, and do not mean to tell it now."

Pasha, as was her habit, did not listen. She went on pressing Tobit, following him about the small room jesting, teasing, threatening, promising. At last Tobit took her by the arm, pulled her to the open door, pushed her out upon the stoop, then slammed and barred the entrance.

Princess Pasha stood there in shock—then shrieked. Screaming and crying, she ran all the way back to the palace where she knew her father was waiting to hear if she had been successful in her quest.

"Pish-posh on the pushing! He hit her!" said Loretta.

"Who cares," said Wynona.

"I do," whimpered Jolene.

"These princesses," continued Wynona in disgust, "set themselves up to be scorned. To hell with their fury. They should go create secrets of their own and make *the men* wonder."

"Shall I continue?" asked Hilda.

"Do!" said the dragons in chorus, all three heads bobbing in a synchronized nod.

"If he had a thousand souls," cried King Wittlesbach when he heard how the common youth had put his ungenteel hands upon a royal princess, "I would starve each of them to death, that son of a dragon!"

The king that very day ordered the summerhouse to be bricked up with Tobit locked inside.

Pasha went out to watch the work, perplexed by the sense of doom rising in her heart. She was having, for the first time in her young life, second thoughts. She wandered to the far side of the cottage where blackberry bushes brushed against a grove of trees. Here she sat and watched the masons lay brick upon brick. To one she began to prattle and jest and he, of course, was very flattered that a princess paid him mind and complimented his work. In the end, as a joke between them, he left three bricks loose. No mortar was spread between three low blocks on one corner, and this left an opening just large enough for a bottle of wine and some food to pass through. Into this opening every morning Princess Pasha passed a hearty breakfast to prisoner Tobit.

Wynona's dragon face was framed in furrows. Hilda surmised she disapproved of the softening of Pasha.

Jolene, in contrast, cooed and sighed through a pasted lipless smile.

Loretta yawned. "What food do you supposed the princess passed through to him?"

Hilda shrugged and continued.

KING WITTLESBACH *of Pannonia was in an ongoing battle of wits with the Sultan of Uman, but the tête-à-tête was all veneer. The underlying conflict was always in danger of spilling onto the battlefield, and the Pannonians were ill-prepared for such a possibility. So when an ambassador arrived from the sultan bearing a riddle, Wittlesbach trembled.*

The silk-clad ambassador presented three finely carved walking sticks, gifts of goodwill. He told King Wittlesbach how all three staffs were carved from the same trunk. The king thanked the ambassador as profusely as he thought culturally appropriate, and told him he regretted having no equal gift to offer in return. The messenger (after stating with vigor that he was under strict orders to come home empty-handed) arose to go as quickly as he had come. But, just as the sultan's servant's second foot was crossing over the throne room threshold, he turned back, bowed low, and added, "My master bids me ask, O Wise King of the West, which of these three canes grew nearest the root, which in the middle, and which high up near the branches."

King Wittlesbach's eyes grew wide as the servant continued, "And if you cannot tell me, perhaps my sultan—may he live forever—is worthy of your daughter after all."

King Wittlesbach, trying to hide his anxiety, took the

walking sticks and scrutinized them. He could not see the slightest difference between them. Still, buying as much time as he dared, he told the sultan's servant that he would have the answer for him the following evening.

When the servant left, King Wittlesbach called for Princess Pasha.

"Pasha, my daughter, you must pack your things," the king said. "You are to wed the Sultan of Uman."

Now before she met Tobit, Pasha would have pretended to resist while her heart rejoiced, for she had always believed that to marry a sultan would make her queen and matriarch in some faraway exotic kingdom. Having met Tobit, she instead became anxious. Pasha begged her father to tell her the cause of his momentous and sudden decision.

King Wittlesbach told Pasha all, even hinting (though not quite admitting) that the sultan's army was far greater than his own.

"Do not despair, my father," said the princess. "We shall find a way to answer the riddle." Her father was not convinced, but found some comfort in the brave words of his daughter.

Pasha took her concerns to Tobit. Through the hole in the bricks she whispered her plight, and through the hole she watched Tobit pace deep in thought. For the first time she noticed his sword and wondered to herself—Why is a prisoner allowed a weapon? And why does it seem to tremble in the scabbard as intensely as the young man thinks?

Tobit stopped in his tracks, and—without so much as a glance in Pasha's direction—gave the following order, "Go to bed as usual," he said, "and when you awaken in the morning, tell your father that you have dreamed that the canes must be placed in warm water. One will sink to the bottom. That is the one that grew nearest the root. One will float in the middle, neither sinking nor coming to the surface. The last, the one cut near the high branches, will float to the top."

The next morning, Pasha told her father of her "dream."

Her father listened and took action.

The sultan's messenger left for home dumbfounded.

The princess told Tobit all the next morning as she brought him a hearty breakfast made by her own hand.

FORTY DAYS LATER, the Sultan of Uman sent his ambassador to Pannonia again. Wittlesbach trembled. The linen-clad ambassador led three foals, all from the same stud, right into the throne room. The king thanked him as profusely as he thought culturally appropriate, and told him he regretted having no equal gift to offer in return. The ambassador (after stating with vigor that King Wittlesbach's presence was present enough) arose to go as quickly as he had come. But, just as the sultan's servant's second foot was crossing over the throne room threshold, he turned back, bowed low, and added, "My master bids me ask, O Wise King of the West, which of these three foals was born in the morning, which at noon, and which at evening?"

King Wittlesbach's eyes grew wide and his heart sank. He did not expect his daughter to be lucky enough to have a second dream of discernment, and his army had grown thinner due to a bad case of the flu.

The servant from Uman pretended not to notice, but Wittlesbach was sure he saw a sneer when the servant bowed again (not quite as low as before) and added, "And if you cannot tell me, perhaps my sultan—may he live forever—is worthy of your daughter after all."

"What's it with human fathers trading daughters?" asked Jolene. "We dragons choose our mates."

"If we do not eat them first," said Wynona with a grin that showed all her pointy teeth.

"What I want to know," interrupted Loretta, "is what is it with the sets of three? Three loose bricks, three sticks, three tender foals."

... and three dragons, thought Hilda to herself.

"Shall I continue?" Hilda asked.

"Do!" said all three dragons in chorus, bobbing their heads as one.

King Wittlesbach took the foals' reins and inspected the animals closely. He could see not the slightest difference between them. Still, buying as much time as he dared, he told the sultan's servant that he would have the answer for him the following evening.

Princess Pasha entered the throne room just as the servant was leaving. She did not like the leering look he gave her and was about to complain to her father, but noted Wittlesbach's gloomy countenance. The king stood, head down, holding the lead ropes of three young horses. "I have yet another challenge from the sultan," he mumbled, not looking up.

Pasha, who had educated herself between the messenger's visits, now understood that the Sultan of Uman had twelve wives already. She would be thirteenth, a very unlucky number.

Pasha answered her father with even more determination than before, "Do not despair, my father. We shall find a way to answer the riddle." Her father was not convinced, but again found much comfort in the brave words of his daughter.

Pasha took her concerns straight to Tobit and, through the hole in the bricks, told him the riddle. She watched Tobit pace, deep in thought once again, the sword vibrating in its scabbard.

Tobit stopped and turned to meet Pasha's stare. Her heart pounded as he spoke. "Go to bed as usual, my dove," he said, "and when night comes, pretend to scream out in your sleep.

Scream so loud that your father hears you and comes running. Inform him that you have dreamt that you were chained to the wall of a harem and ... do not say more. Just imply ..."

Pasha nodded.

"Next, tell your father that you will be made an inglorious concubine instead of a majestic queen, your rightful destiny. Tell him that this is your fate only because no one would listen to the young man shut up in the summerhouse. Tell the king his prisoner holds the answer to the riddle of the foals."

Pasha obeyed and, before dawn, Tobit stood before the King Wittlesbach.

[5]

TOBIT GOES TO UMAN

They say disasters come in threes
I know of only one
But Sorrow now abides in me
And you have just begun

I did not expect you to still be alive," said His Majesty when Tobit stood before him, "but I trust you used your time in the summerhouse to repent of your wicked conduct. I grant you pardon on the condition that you help me solve a riddle."

Tobit nodded and the king told him the conundrum.

"Yes, I can help you," said Tobit, "but let us discuss the answer outside. Having been so long confined, I need to stand under open sky." The king followed the freed prisoner, trying not to seem too eager.

Stretching his arms out and looking upward, Tobit commanded, "Bring me three identical troughs. Fill one with oats, one with wheat, and one with barley. The horse that eats the oats was foaled in the morning, the horse that eats the wheat was *foaled at noon, and the horse that eats the barley was foaled at night."*

That evening, the messenger of Uman left dumbfounded. Reaching home he was at once deprived of the opportunity to deliver a third enigma, for as soon as the sultan saw his servant return without a thirteenth royal bride, the ambassador was thrown into prison.

FOR A DAY, *the Sultan of Uman found nothing to do but sulk. His wicked servant had failed to ensure political dominance through the only eligible Pannonian princess. On day two, the sultan's mood became so sour that he sent for his auntie.*

Auntie Maximilla was a housekeeper for three mountain dragons who gave her leave to go, on the condition that there was plenty left in the pot for them to sup on.

"Lizardly landlords?" interrupted Wynona. "Is that how you humans describe us? Are we a joke?"

"You commanded me, ma'am, to leave out nothing, to tell tales just as my mother and her mother told them," answered Hilda trembling inside.

Wynona's eyes narrowed but she made no answer.

"Humans really call us lizards ..." mused Jolene, in rhetorical wonderment.

"Well, it is pitiful," said Wynona to her companions, "but proof that the young one is not changing things for her audience, just telling as she heard it. I had half a mind to eat her but must admit she is doing precisely as I asked."

"At least dragons have entered the story," added Jolene, "however ridiculous and inaccurate."

"I wonder what Auntie Maximilla left in the pot for her masters," said Loretta.

"Shall I continue?" asked Hilda.

"Do!" said all three dragons together.

"It is not King Wittlesbach who has answered your riddles," said Auntie Maximilla when her nephew told his story. "The King of Pannonia is far too stupid, and his daughter has just begun to use her mind. I will consult the dragon's eye, for another soul is interfering with the age-old forces that govern the battle of wits between Pannonia and Uman."

"Dragon's eye?" said Wynona, cutting Hilda off before she found her rhythm again. "What the

frack is a dragon's eye?"

"It will be explained soon, I promise, if I may continue ..." Hilda answered, almost showing her frustration. She had never told stories under duress before and constant interruption was wearing on her nerves.

"Go on, go on," said Wynona, "I'll try to bite my bifurcated tongue."

Auntie Maximilla left, and returned four days later with an answer. It was a difficult and puzzling one, but at least it gave a hint of direction. Of course, Auntie had to present it as a rhyme for, though she had settled her lot in life as a maidservant for dragons, she had always wanted to be a full-fledged sorceress. Rhymes were as close as she could come to conjuring spells—

> **She loves a youth from far away**
> **Who solved your riddles, both**
> > **one and two**
> **Her father will trade his soul**
> > **for peace**
> **Insist the lad be sent to you**

The sultan, a stickler for grammar, wanted to stop and insist that Auntie Maximilla clarify whose soul was being traded for peace, the king's or the youth's. But he thought it wise to spare the poetess's feelings and followed the context clues. He sent a message that very day demanding a certain mysterious youth be sent from Pannonia to Uman for the sake of cultural exchange.

By the time King Wittlesbach received the message from the Sultan of Uman (noting with interest that it was not delivered by the same messenger) he no longer hated Tobit. In fact, he was growing rather attached to the young man. Attached enough, in fact, that he did not want to part with him. But King Wittlesbach had just quit shuddering from his daughter's hysterical description of being chained in a harem, and there was a degree of relief that the price of peace was Tobit, not Pasha.

Tobit read King Wittlesbach troubled face and stepped forward. "Do not fear, sire," he said, "to Uman I am destined to go. Only send with me two more youths near my age and stature, and dress us all alike. I assure you, either the two of them will return to you wiser, or all three of us shall come back to Pannonia unscathed."

The sword dizzied itself spinning in approval. Princess Pasha swooned.

Wynona and Jolene snickered.

W*HEN* T*OBIT and the two youths arrived in Uman, there was none to point out who was whom. The servant messenger, twice sent to Pannonia, had perished in the sultan's prison. Something about forgetting to feed him was the excuse given by the warden.*

Along their journey, Tobit trained his companions in mimicry. By the time they reached their destination, all three youths' mannerisms, gestures, and timber of voice were so alike that Auntie Maximilla could not choose which young man she needed to condemn. The dragon's eye she claimed to consult was no more than old woman's intuition (and the occasional favor of her landlords, who threw her a tip when their supper was particularly satisfying).

"Aah," interjected Wynona. "The dynamic is making a bit more sense. Go on."

"Does this story footnote the recipes?" said Loretta.

It was Jolene's turn then to jam her elbow in a sister dragon's ribs.

When the three young men entered the sultan's throne room, he made a sign for them to come near. They all bowed low in greeting, in one motion, at the same angle. He asked them about their journey and they answered in one voice. That night at dinner the three sat together, rose together, chewed and swallowed together in complete synchronization. It was unnerving. The sultan could not detect any difference between the three youths; neither could he bring himself to kill or hold all three captive.

Noting his auntie's loss of bravado, the sultan felt even more irritated that he had allowed his ambassador to perish in prison. The emotion bordered on remorse, and the feeling, so new to him, was difficult to process. The three guests were playing the part of "cultural exchange" to the T. What excuse could be found for harming them?

The next morning the sultan, now tired of the whole affair, began thinking perhaps twelve wives were enough and that the Kingdom of Uman needed no further expansion. He allowed Auntie Maximilla to make one final address to the three guests before he sent them on their way. He expected her to shout threats or weave rhymes, but Auntie did neither. Auntie Maximilla decided instead to gamble.

"Three honored guests," she began. "By spells and charms I had heard of an amazing youth in the land of Pannonia. I asked

my nephew, the sultan, to bid him come as a personal favor to me. I cannot tell you how surprised and pleased I am to find there is not one superior male specimen from the west, but three." Auntie bowed low to Tobit and his friends and went on, "Three noble youths, would you help an old woman? For the problem I face is threefold and you, a threefold solution, bode well."

Tobit pricked his ears, paying close attention to her every syllable, gesture, and inflection. His companions did their best to mirror him. Auntie, who was equally attentive, thought she saw that only one of the three youths' swords shook in its scabbard as she continued her appeal. "My house is infested by three dragons and, though it has been within my power to tame them, neither I nor any man of Uman can chase them out. I have grown weary of living and sleeping, cooking and cleaning, all the while in constant danger. I begged my nephew for help and have found favor in his eyes. He, the Sultan of Uman, has agreed to live in peace with Pannonia, not asking for daughters, nor lands, nor sending endless riddles to vex your king if ... and only if ... the three dragons are slain."

Two things occurred next, one just as Auntie expected and one to her great surprise. First, which youth was the one sought after became crystal clear. Tobit stood taller while his companions shrank. Second, Tobit called out, with no hesitation nor excuse for delay, "Show me the great lizards! I will defeat them, one against three."

"Now that," exclaimed Loretta, "is a clever woman! Getting her problems solved with someone else's brawn. Auntie is playing the men like violins! Next she'll rile up her housemates and send them out to do her dirty work! Of course I wish she wasn't using dragons as pawns in her clever scheme, but what a woman!"

"Don't trust a human story, Loretta dear," countered

Wynona, "It rarely turns out well for our kind. We are here to learn. Like relations between Uman and Pannonia, it is a cultural exchange."

"Humph!" said Loretta. "It's three dragons against one neophyte."

"Shall I continue?" asked Hilda.

"Do," said all three together.

Auntie Maximilla prostrated herself before the sultan to show gratitude, but smiled widely under her matted hair. The youth she was after was exposed and, in his eagerness, as good as dead.

The sultan shook his head in admiration of both Tobit's naive bravery and his aunt's subtle craft. To assuage what was left of his remorse, he ordered the two sidekicks to be well-supplied, packed off, and sent home. Two out of three returning would send the necessary message, and leave the Pannonian king shaking in his cheaply made second-rate boots.

TOBIT'S SWORD UNSHEATHED

Distract the pain
Beyond all reach
Pass the time
and do not teach
O frabjous day! Callooh! Callay!
Just entertain
and do not preach

Auntie Maximilla herself guided Tobit to her little home deep inside the neighboring forest. She had him wait just outside her garden gate on a patch of encroaching crabgrass, perfectly suited to be set aflame. She proceeded inside, promising to send the dragons out to meet him in short order.

Closing the door behind her, Maximilla called to the great serpents Meeney, Miney, and Mo, "Remember how you promised to raise my salary if I brought you fresh knight? Well, peek out the window and see one young and tender, waiting with eagerness to meet the three of you."

"Are you sure her name is not Aunt Eeny?" quipped Wynona with a small smile.

"Hush! It's finally getting good," said Loretta, licking her lips.

"I'm telling it as I heard it," said Hilda, and she pressed on.

Meeney, Miney, and Mo peered out the window and smiled. Identical sets of jagged glimmering teeth flashed in anticipation.

"Remember to share," admonished Auntie Maximilla with a chuckle as they slithered out to meet the waiting guest.

Tobit saw the dragons coming, undulating and flexing, mighty to behold.

He did not budge, he did not blink, and when three heads darted forth in the same split second, so did Tobit's sword.

Each head was cut off in the quick succession.

"Well I guess it was an actual sword after all!" exclaimed Jolene.

The other two listeners held their tongues, but Hilda noted the dropped jaws. She grew worried. "Shall I continue? The story is kind of upsetting for a dragon audience ... I can change it if you'd like."

"Do NOT!" screamed Wynona, "change a single detail! I will not flinch in the face of human fabrications. Give it to us straight, like I asked!"

Hilda was sure she saw a little spurt of flame with the outburst. Her heart skipped a fearful beat but she proceeded on.

The feat of daring happened with such speed that Auntie Maximilla, who had gone to the kitchen to put on the kettle, did not notice until an eerie silence invaded. She did not hear the thump, thump, thump as the bodies of Meeney, Miney, and Mo fell to ground. Not a blade of crabgrass was harmed. The crashing carcasses fell instead upon the newly blooming bego-

nias, smashing them. Maximilla did not see Tobit gather the dragon's heads and skewer them like shish kababs.

Neither the sultan nor his aunt knew that Tobit slipped silently away to the city streets of Uman. There he traded a single dragon's tooth for a fine suit of clothes and a royal charger upon which to ride home. They did, however, discover within the week that three dragon's heads were set upon poles at the border between Pannonia and Uman. No army dared cross over as long as Meeney, Miney, and Mo looked down, and dragon's heads take two generations to decompose.

"Is that true?" asked Jolene, looking at her fellow listeners. Hilda opened her mouth ready to once again defend the veracity of the tale, then realized it was not to her that the question was addressed.

"Our body parts are valuable in human commerce," said Loretta.

"I mean about the decay," said Jolene. "Dragon's heads on poles for generations ..."

"It seems," said Wynona, "We can cull a few lessons from the fable: one—dragons, dead and alive, strike fear in the heart of man. Two—dragon remains weigh more with peoples than does gold. As for decomposition, save the question for Geraldine. She will know."

All three listeners sat quiet for a long spell. Hilda broke the silence at last, continuing on as if there had been no upset.

As the days slipped by and Tobit did not return, Princess Pasha passed her nights in despair. When his two fellow travelers crept through the palace gates without him, her tears turned to resolve. That very day, she began to pester her father to give her troops to command. Surprised but proud, King Wittlesbach capitulated.

In front of a thin band of soldiers Princess Pasha rode, dressed in uniform.

"That is a blatant modernization," interjected Wynona.

"I tell it the way my grandmother told it," said Hilda.

Wynona waved a backhanded claw for her to proceed. Hilda did, but noted all three listeners seemed disheartened, less zealous. She feared her audience was growing disengaged.

The princess had not gone more than ten miles when Tobit came riding forth to meet her. She lifted up her eyes to see the man she loved back from the dead. Springing off her horse she ran on foot to meet him. Tobit swept Pasha in front of him on his charger and the two rode back in triumph.

Upon their arrival, King Wittlesbach declared that Tobit would be his son-in-law as soon as wedding preparations could be made. He also declared for himself an early retirement from the throne. Tobit would be king when he returned from his honeymoon.

Three days later, the wedding ceremony was performed. That night, out together under the stars, Tobit turned to Pasha and said, "O love of my heart, would you like to know my secret now?"

And Pasha laughed until she cried, saying, "I had forgotten, my king, that I ever wanted to know."

"I will tell you anyhow. And when my mother arrives this spring—for I have sent for her—you will make known to her what I am about to tell you. She surpassed all in her curiosity regarding the matter."

Queen Pasha nodded, surprised she did not mind in the least about the coming of a mother-in-law. Her husband continued, "I dreamt when I was a little boy, sleeping in the sun out in my mother's garden, that I should become King of Pannonia. If my mother had not beaten me to know the secret, it would never have come true."

And so the story ended. Human audiences would have clapped.

Hilda received no adulation, only shocked silence.

She stood and curtsied, asking, "May I bring my guests more refreshments?"

All three heads shook "no."

"Well," Hilda said, "as Miss Wynona insightfully pointed out, I, a poor girl-human, have to eat much more often than dragons do. So if you will excuse me ..."

All three waved her away towards the cabin.

Halfway to the door, a voice called out through the darkening twilight, "But we insist you return once you dine. We require more stories."

[7]

THELMA, THIA, AND THEKLA

A shirt, some shoes
Some silver slacks
And golden buttons
Are all he lacks
All her teeth
And uncrossed eyes
She cooks, she sews
At least she tries

Hilda took a deep breath when she reentered the cabin, then exhaled in the sweetness of familiar surroundings. The thought of being alone, which had haunted her earlier that day, now seemed wondrous. Knowing she would need her strength, she forced herself to eat several bites of jerky though she felt no hunger. Story after story might still be demanded of her.

She did not tarry too long, wanting to return before a dragon summoned her. For though her guests were beginning to treat her as a servant, she was determined to play the part of hostess. Hostesses did not leave their guests unattended. Hilda took a long slow drink of ale. Straightening her dress and re-braiding her long chestnut hair, she stepped back out into the fray.

When the young woman retook her seat among dragons, she had thought this time to bring a blanket for warmth and cushion against the cold stone. Her three guests, talking among themselves, neither paused nor altered their conversation when she rejoined them.

The fire needed no tending, so she sat, hands folded, and waited.

"I still say," Loretta was asserting, "that if Geraldine were here she would NOT have moaned over the loss of three adolescent ninny muffins, dependent on an old biddy. Some of our kind never do grow up if they aren't forced to."

"That is not my point," shot back Wynona. "Of course Geraldine wouldn't care about the three fools cared for by Auntie Maximilla. I was only saying it was interesting how there were only two human matrons in the story and they were both sorry pieces of work. One old wench pampered dragons who never grew up. The other tortured Tobit. And though I have no affinity for a dragon murderer, mind you, he had no proper mothering. This could very well be the people-given excuse for the young man's violent nature."

All eyes now turned towards Hilda.

"Do you have, my dear, any stories with proper mothers?" said Jolene, voice dripping.

"And don't drop out the dragons, of course," growled Wynona, "that goes without saying."

Hilda understood both what was stated and what was left unsaid. In the next story she chose it would be best for not a single dragon to meet with a violent end. But the two parameters—a good mother and the survival of dragons—limited her array of choices. *And* Wynona had expressly forbade the changing of cannon.

Hilda stood, paced, poked the fire. Genuine lore in which dragons were not slain was scarce. Tales with a nurturing mother were scarcer still. Combining the two limitations narrowed her mental search down to one possibility, and it would have to be tweaked on the fly. Hilda hoped Wynona would be too enthralled to notice.

"Enough fidgeting and prodding, young human," said Loretta with an impatient undercurrent. "We know how to keep a flame going. You tell us another tale."

Hilda sat, took a huge breath, and began.

ONCE UPON A TIME *there lived an emperor who had half a world all to himself. On the edges of his eastern wilderness dwelt a widowed shepherdess with three daughters—Thelma, Thia, and Thekla.*

Thelma, the eldest, was so beautiful that when she took the sheep to pasture, they forgot to eat. Thia, the second, was so beautiful that when she was driving the flock, the wolves protected the sheep. But Thekla, the youngest, with hair as soft as the finest lamb's wool, was as beautiful as both her sisters put together.

One summer day, when the rays of the sun were pouring down on the earth, the three sisters went to the woods to pick strawberries.

"Three beauties," sighed Jolene. "Like us."

"A couple centuries and it fades," quipped Wynona. "Do you have anything to fall back on?"

Jolene scowled.

"How big were the strawberries, Hilda?" said Loretta. "Were they ripe and red and dripping with juice?"

"I don't know. But I suppose they could be. Miss Wynona, do you mind a small change for Miss Loretta?"

Wynona rolled her eyes and breathed a barely audible, "Whatever."

As the three sisters gathered plump strawberries—red and ripe and bursting with nectar—they heard the tramp of horses approaching. The girls were so used to the quiet of the hills that they thought a whole army was riding by, but it was only the emperor going to hunt with a handful of his trusted attendants. All were fine handsome men, who rode upon their horses as if they were part of them, but the finest and handsomest of all was the young emperor himself.

As the entourage drew near to the three sisters, the hunting party noticed their beauty, and reined in their horses to ride by at the slowest pace possible.

"Listen, sisters!" whispered Thelma as they passed. "If one of those young men should make me his wife, I would bake him a loaf of bread that would keep him young and brave even as he advanced in years."

"And if I," said Thia almost inaudibly, "should be chosen, I would weave my husband a shirt that would keep him unscathed when he goes to battle, undrenched when traveling through water, and unscorched when passing through dragon's fire."

"And I," said Thekla, "would give the man who chooses me two boys, twins, each with a golden star on his forehead, as bright as those in the eastern sky."

Though the sisters spoke low, the young men heard, and turned their horses' heads.

To Thekla's surprise, the emperor himself took note and, before she had time to draw breath, he swung her on his saddle before him, saying, "I take you at your word. You are chosen, my lovely future empress!"

"And I will have you," said a strapping young man to Thelma.

"And I you," exclaimed another to Thia.

"Exterior beauty standards even applied to the males," said Wynona. "Like a trio of peacocks."

"Dreamy ..." sighed Jolene.

"Did the girls spill the baskets of strawberries? Are they taking the berries along?" Loretta wanted to know.

"Shall I continue?" asked Hilda.

"Do!"

All the horses were now turned back towards the palace. Thekla knew their mother would cry, sitting at supper alone, and she wished to bid her goodbye and gain her blessing. But it was the emperor's saddle she rode upon now, and who was she to instruct him?

In less than a week, the marriages took place, and for three days and three nights there was nothing but feasting as the news spread over the whole kingdom.

When the rejoicings ended, Thelma sent for corn. In the presence of all, she made from it the loaf she had promised at the strawberry beds.

Next Thia sent for flax, dried it, spun it, and wove it into linen. To the amazement of the watching courtiers, sewed the shirt she had promised at the strawberry beds.

Thekla's promise of twins (a guarantee that could not be fulfilled in the presence of all) required patience. She was thankful to find the emperor was as loving and kind as the father she remembered. He insisted she call him by his first name, Cormac, instead of Lord Most High Emperor Husband, as was tradition.

"How kind of him," hissed Wynona through gritted teeth, "and how is it human women allow themselves to be lowered thus? Sister one cooks, sister two sews, sister three promises babies. We dragons are not chattel."

"Isn't it beautiful?" interrupted Jolene, not processing a single one of Wynona's words. "And each girl will be made rapturous by a husband who adores her. I wish we dragons had more happily-ever-afters."

Loretta, while wondering to herself how magic bread might taste, voiced a concern of a relational nature. "Thekla, the youngest, has been chosen by the emperor, we shall hear plenty about her. But, I would bet my eye-fangs that we will hear not a word more about Thelma and Thia. The middle-born will be shoved aside. It is the way of the peoples to do so according to birth order. Yet Thelma will also fade—first-born AND a cook! It makes no sense! Yet, mark my word, we will hear no more about her and her baking exploits."

All three fell silent. Hilda found it befuddling that each dragon, having now spoken her mind, seemed to possess something akin to contentment. None seemed to recognize the dearth of feedback. They craved no more than what was offered. Sputtering disjointed speeches counted as communication. It was very human.

"Shall I?" asked Hilda.

"Go on, go on."

Emperor Cormac's father, like Thekla's, had died long ago. He too had left behind a widow. Cormac's stepmother insisted Thekla call her Mother Nefary, instead of Most High Glorious Dowager, as was tradition (or so she said).

Mother Nefary had a daughter, Princess Perfidy, by her first husband (a lower duke). She had always dreamed that her daughter would be empress one day. With all her heart she hated Thekla, the child of a mere shepherd, but could do nothing under the watchful eye of Emperor Cormac.

To unsettle the placid calm of the palace, Princess Perfidy and Mother Nefary began to spread rumors. Soon all in residence whispered of a dragon roaming the outskirts of the kingdom, besieging small frontier towns and eating up livestock. The young emperor sprang up in wrath the moment he heard the news, vowing that nothing should hinder his giving battle. Thekla suspected something was amiss but also feared. If a dragon were truly afoot, her aging mother might be in harm's way.

Cormac assembled a cadre of soldiers and set off at once to meet the beast. Much to the tale-bearing women's surprise, there was indeed a dragon traumatizing the citizenry on the frontier. But before Emperor Cormac had the satisfaction of running it through with his lance, the beast laughed merrily and flew away.

"Sounds like a Zendino to me," muttered Wynona. Only Hilda heard and sighed inside with relief. The fact that Wynona was guessing at speciation, rather than scrutinizing for any deviation from canon, eased her anxiety. The laughing dragon flying away from Emperor Cormac was not a part of oral tradition ... until now.

[8]

TWO WITH STARS

Only the aspen and old beech know
Whatever wife and daughter say
What direction the cold winds blow
All blowback is but delay

*D*uring the weeks the emperor was away, early in the morning when stars grow pale in the sky two little boys with golden hair were born. Each had a star on his forehead. Thekla, much exhausted and just escaping death, had not noticed Mother Nefary had insisted on playing midwife. The cruel woman took the babes as soon as they were born, and, with her own hand, dug two graves. She buried both of the emperor's newborn sons right outside the palace under his bedroom window.

Into the bassinet, Nefary placed instead two large golden salamanders.

"Double frack. You peoples overdo the evil stepmother genre," yawned Loretta. "I thought this story was supposed to contain proper mothering."

"The girls did have a good mother at the beginning, remember?" said Jolene.

"Where the flaggnard is she now?" said Loretta.

"It will be explained soon, I promise," answered Hilda, stamping her foot.

"Sorry, I'll shut up and listen," said Loretta, making a show of biting her tongue.

As Cormac road back towards home, news reached him that his wife had given birth. Straightway he galloped full speed to the palace and bounded up the stairs to Thekla's room. He was happy at first to see his wife alive, but all pleasure was consumed in horror when he looked upon the contents of the bassinet.

Nefary and Perfidy, feigning great sorrow, produced streams of crocodile tears, mourning the insanity of Empress Thekla. "Oh what a horrible twist to the promise she made at the strawberry beds!" they wailed. "How the heart of the emperor must be torn!"

The emperor's heart was at first torn indeed, but then it grew cold and hard. He recalled how Thekla's sisters had kept their promises of a loaf of bread and flaxen shirt. And his bitter disappointment was compounded by the fact that his betrayal seemed somehow foretold in the way the dragon, with its golden skin and slanting eyes, had laughed at him. He gave orders for his wife to be put out of the kingdom. He could no longer bear to look upon her.

Perfidy kissed the ring of the king and offered herself as solace.

Cormac, mind darkened, took up the offer of comfort.

Nefary exulted.

In a single day, all the Most High Glorious Dowager's wishes had been fulfilled. She took personal charge of Thekla's punishment and had her buried out in the wilderness up to her neck. By this, she declared, every citizen would know what happens to those who dare to deceive the emperor. Thekla's sisters, Thelma and Thia, longed to go and give her aid and comfort, but each was prevented by her husband. Each man had sworn obedience to the Lord Most High Emperor. His enemies were theirs.

"I would never abandon you, sister," Jolene sniffled to Loretta.

Loretta rolled her eyes and breathed a barely audible, "Whatever."

Under their father *the emperor's window, the poor little baby boys found no rest in their graves. In the spot where each was buried sprang up two beautiful young aspens. Nefary hated the sight of the trees for they ate at what remained of her conscience. She gave orders that the trees should be uprooted, but the emperor heard of it, and forbade them to be touched. He sighed in the midst of his command, "Let them alone. They are the finest aspens I have ever seen."*

The trees grew as no aspens had ever grown before. Each day and night added one year's maturation, and at dawn, when the stars faded out of the sky, they grew a foot in the twinkling of an eye. As their branches swept across the palace windows, and the wind moved them softly, the emperor would sit, and listen, and grow peaceful with melancholy.

Nefary was bent on destroying the aspens, and though a woman's will can squeeze blood out of a turnip, her cunning was thwarted by the king's love of the trees. Nefary turned to her daughter to employ soft words of coaxing instead. Perfidy was well trained in the use of feminine tears.

Empress Perfidy sat on the edge of the wide soft bed she

shared with Cormac, and began to entreat him with a purring voice: how an allergy to aspens bothered her, how the view from the palace was blocked, how she imagined their future children running in the space taken up by the ever-thickening trunks.

Cormac refused. Cormac ignored. But emperors are only men, and, in the end, Cormac caved. At last, exasperated, he blurted, "Have your way. Cut down the trees. But out of one shall be made a wooden bed frame for me, and out of the other, a second and separate bed for you."

The aspens were cut down the next morning, and by evening beds made of their timber were placed in separate royal chambers.

"Classic mistake," said Wynona. "Human female fool! To spend one's power for the making of a bed and losing the power of sharing that very bed in the process. Congratulations, Perfidy, you won a battle and are now weaponless in the war."

Hilda did not understand and sat in silence.

Loretta understood but cared very little.

Jolene did not want to understand but cared very much. "Go on with the story," she said in irritation. "It feels so sad and I must find out what happens."

That night, when Cormac lay down in his new bed, he felt he had grown a hundred times heavier. With the great weightiness came a calm that was quite new to him. Perfidy, in contrast, felt as if she were laying on thorns and nettles. She had to snatch an hour or two of broken sleep upon the floorboards.

In his new bed, the Emperor Cormac had dreams in a language he could barely understand. A small voice called from a distance down the hall, "Is he too heavy for you, little brother?" And a voice nearby, so close it seemed in the bedroom, answered "Oh, no, he is not heavy at all. I feel nothing but joy now that our beloved father rests over me."

Later in the night the nearby voice called out, "How goes it for you, my brother?" And the same distant voice answered back, "Her evil soul is very heavy for me! I am thankful she paces most of the night and sinks often to lie upon the floor."

[9]

HILDA UNINTERRUPTED

One fish two fish
Golden new fish
Examine every shimmering scale
Sparkling bright from head to tail

Within the week, Perfidy was determined to get rid of the beds. She had two others identical in every measure made, and on a day that the emperor had gone hunting, she placed them instead in their rooms. The offensive aspen beds were burnt in a large bonfire behind the stables, until only a little heap of ashes remained.

Nefary stood by her daughter and watched the aspen burn. When the fire died away, the two stooped, gathered up the ashes, and scattered them to the four winds. Neither woman noticed that where the fire burnt brightest two sparks flew up, looming above them in the air for a few moments, then floated down into the great river that flowed through the heart of the country. Here the sparks turned into two little fishes, exact in form down to the detail of each golden scale.

The next morning, the emperor's fishermen went down to the river to catch fish for their master's breakfast. They cast into the stream just as the last star twinkled out of the morning sky. Among the multitude of fish they drew in, two were covered in golden scales such as no man had ever looked upon.

All the fishermen gathered round and wondered at the beauty of the twin fishes. After some discussion, they decided that they would keep them alive to give as a present to the emperor. To their surprise the fishes spoke to this suggestion with one voice, "Do not take us to the palace, for that is where we came from. To return would be our destruction."

Upon these words, the men drew back, seeing that fearful sorcery was at play. Only one courageous fisherman leaned in to ask, "What are we to do with you, then?"

The fishes gave clear and specific instruction as the fisherman took notes: "There is a young shepherdess abiding with her aged mother along the eastern wilderness. She never smiles, but if you speak to her of twin golden fishes, she will grow radiant and give you a lock of her hair. Soak her long tresses in the morning dew, lay the two of us in the sun, and then circle the lock round us tip to end. Do not come near again until the sun's rays have had time to dry our mother's hair."

The group of fishermen, glad to support their friend's brave and strange endeavor, agreed to tend his nets while he attempted this most unusual quest. The man did as he was instructed and the journey unfolded just as the fishes predicted. The only surprise was that after her initial jubilation, tears flowed from the woman's eyes as she cut her long hair. Also strange (at least to the fisherman) was her silence. Never before had he met a woman who had nothing to say.

By the time the traveling fisherman returned to the golden twins, he could not tell if the lock held more tears or more dew. He had done his best to gather condensation from the leaves he had passed by on the way back home. All he knew, in truth, was that he had done his best to follow instructions.

T HE FISHERMAN'S *efforts produced an amazing effect. When the sun burned hot that afternoon, he went to where he had lain the ring of hair and, instead of fins and scales, he found two beautiful baby boys with golden hair and golden stars gleaming on their foreheads. Each was so like the other that the fisherman's wife, who took them into her care, could not tell them apart.*

The boys grew as no boys had ever grown before. Each day and night added one year's maturation, and at dawn, when the stars faded out of the sky, they grew a foot in the twinkling of an eye. As their height increased, so did their wisdom and knowledge. When three days and three nights had passed they were twelve years in age, twenty-four in strength, and thirty-six in wisdom.

"Kind fisherman," the two said one morning, "We must now go to our father." The fisherman nodded for he had nothing to say about the matter.

Each lad donned a cap made of lambskin sewn by the fisherman's wife that hid the golden hair and stars upon their foreheads. Thus disguised, they headed towards the palace.

[10]

SOME PROPER MOTHERING

We sang to you, father,
from bark of the tree
From bedpost as ashes
flowing down to the sea

It was dinnertime when the twins arrived at their father's home. In spite of the porter's attempts to bar their entry, the two youths pushed through and made their way to a large hall where the emperor was dining surrounded by his court.

"We desire audience," said one prince to a servant standing near the door.

"Quite impossible," huffed the servant.

"Is it? Let us see!" said the second prince, pushing forward.

"What is the matter?" demanded Emperor Cormac, glaring up and across the room from his favorite dish.

The princes stopped as if frozen at the sound of their father's voice.

"It is two boys," called out the dining hall butler, "who want to force their way in!"

*"To **force** their way in? Who dares use force in my palace? What boys are they?" said the emperor all in one breath, growing red with anger. "Thrust them out! Set the dogs after them!"*

"Leave us alone. We will go," said the princes. Both stepped backwards, cut to the heart by Cormac's harsh words. They turned to depart.

"Why?" whispered Jolcnc.

"Why what?" asked Hilda.

Jolene went silent so Loretta filled in her sister's thoughts, "Why were they cut to the heart? The emperor neither knew nor loved them."

"He is their father whether he knows it or not ..." began Hilda.

"So?" said Loretta. "I do not see how, in any of this, the twins could know or love either father or mother. How are they connected or attached to either when deprived of both? Does not a wish of the heart die when it is not fulfilled? How do the tree-boys turned fish-twins have a concept of either parent? This tale is complete nonsense."

Loretta crossed her short arms, hawked a loogie, and launched it into the fire. The flames danced, well-fed.

Wynona sneered, "It is a weakness of the warm-blooded, to have a taste for things they can't even name. Theirs is the way of bitter dissatisfaction—to crave more than what is offered, to want validation from those who sired and birthed them. Then young grow up and birth their own whelps, hoping to extract through parenthood what still feels lacking. Parents live through offspring, offspring resent parents.

"Glean another lesson, lady dragons—be glad for your base ability to hatch and crawl out on your own. Peoples are crippled for life, chasing after the wind. Not so the mighty dragon."

Wynona had stood to finish her speech. She looked round at her staring audience, and slumped back down into her seat.

She seemed to Hilda all at once self-conscious, at least for a dragon.

"Shall I go on now?" said Hilda.

Wynona nodded.

The twin princes had almost exited the emperor's gates when their soft answer struck a chord on their father's heart, resonating with the memories of the aspen trees. A servant was sent in great haste, and the two were brought back. This time their entrance was not blocked. They were ushered in to where their father sat at the head of a long table covered with flowers and filled with guests. Beside him sat Empress Perfidy supported by twelve cushions.

When the princes entered, one of the cushions fell down to the floor, and there remained only eleven.

"Take off your caps," ordered one of the courtiers.

"A covered head is, to some, a sign of honor," replied the boys.

The crowd gasped at the brazenness of the two, but the emperor motioned everyone still. His heart had lost all anger in the golden tones of the boys' voices. A great weightiness came upon him, and with it a calm he could not understand. "Stay as you are, but tell me your names. Where do you come from? What do you want?"

"We are two shoots from one stem," came their answer. "One shoot was broken and buried in the eastern wilderness. The other sits at the head of this table."

The king's brow furrowed but he motioned for the two to continue.

"We have travelled a long way, we have spoken in the rustle of the wind, we have whispered in the wood, we have sung in the waters. But now we wish to tell you a story in the speech of men."

A second cushion fell from under the mighty rumpus of

Empress Perfidy. "Let them take their impudent idiocy home," she ordered for all to hear.

"Oh, no, let them go on," said Emperor Cormac. "Speak, boys. Sing or say to us your story in the speech of men."

In strange chanting harmonies, the princes outlined the story of their lives—

> **There was once a king**
> **Who pulled a young maid**
> **Out from the strawberry fields**
> **He sought neither motherly**
> **blessing nor nod**
> **What could the maid do, but to**
> **yield?**

Two more cushions fell down. And the boys continued—

> **One promise kept—a loaf made**
> **from scratch**
> **Two promises kept—new shirt**
> **made from flax**
> **A third promise kept out of**
> **view of the throng**
> **Treachery, envy, wrong upon**
> **wrong**

Three cushions fell. The boys continued—

> **We sang to you, father, from**
> **bark of the tree**
> **From bedpost as ashes flowing**
> **down to the sea**

> *Our mother was buried still*
> * alive in the soil*
> *You asked not you sought*
> * naught, but remained in the*
> * coils*
> *Not of the dragon, who laughed*
> * and then fled*
> *But the woman who offered you*
> * comfort in bed*

Four more cushions fell to the floor, leaving only one. Seeing this, the two princes repeated the initial lines—

> *There was once a king*
> *Who pulled a young maid*
> *Out from the strawberry fields*
> *...*

The performance was interrupted by Perfidy jumping to her feet. As the last cushion fell to the floor, the twins lifted their caps, showing golden hair and stars upon their foreheads. The eyes of the emperor and of all his guests were so bent on them that the two young men shrank under the intensity of attention. Both walked backwards towards the door.

Such a tumult arose that not many noticed the visitors had slipped from the palace. The screeching of the empress was enough to pierce eardrums.

"Well cuss that poor she-devil," interrupted Wynona. "I knew she was a lost cause, but I had hoped for more dignity from her."

"I know that screech," said Loretta, wincing. "It rang in my eardrums all through my hatchling days … what happened to the wench of an empress, Miss Hilda?"

"Some say she was demoted to a scullery maid," said Hilda. "Others say she screamed until her heart burst, or she threw herself off a cliff. There is little agreement, so I do not usually include that part. Would you like me to add one of the many options in my telling?

"Screw her," said Wynona.

Jolene, unlike her companions, remained quiet. There was nothing for Hilda to do but finish the plot.

ONCE OUTSIDE THE PALACE, *the twins turned to walk eastward. Halfway to their destination, under the light of a full moon, their father caught up with them. He rode alone with the reins of two additional mounts in his hand. With horses under them the three continued on, neither stopping nor speaking until they came to the spot where Empress Thekla had been buried up to her neck.*

It was here, years before, that Thekla's mother had found her half-dead. It was here, not long after, that Thekla repented leaving her home without a word and was forgiven. It was here, that very morning, that Thekla had buried her old mother and found herself all alone in the world. The men dismounted and ran their fingers through the soft earth of a new grave.

Thekla stood under the shadow of a nearby beech, long dusky shadows hiding her from view as she watched her three loves ride up. Now she walked out to join her two sons and her husband where they knelt. And here, upon his mother-in-law's grave, Emperor Cormac begged for forgiveness from the strawberry maid who had enamored him with a beautiful promise—a promise she had kept.

Thekla nodded but did not speak. But when Cormac swung

her on the saddle before him, and the four rode westwardly back
towards the palace, she sang a song her mother once sang.

Hilda stood now. She had heard the tune from her grandmother's own lips and felt as if the old lady, long passed away,
was singing through her. She now, for the first time, knew why
and how these particular lyrics latched on to the end of
Thekla's tale. The reptilian audience stared and listened as the
young maiden looked up at the stars and rendered a melody
clear and sweet—

> ***My four go out from me to play***
> ***Bags packed I send them on***
> >   ***their way.***
> ***Sent out from me, apart***
> >   ***from me***
> ***Derived from me and wrought***
> ***Within my skin, blood and***
> >   ***bone,***
> ***My very own, yet not***
> ***My teachers, yet by me once***
> >   ***taught***
> ***Love ties to home in upward***
> >   ***growing***
> ***Down to a silent shrouded***
> >   ***knowing***
> ***Soul to soul***
> ***Soul to soul***
> ***The more I loose you all***
> >   ***my four***
> ***Entwined our lives grow all***
> >   ***the more***
> ***Fly back through the open door***

the always open door.

Emperor Cormac, for the first time attuned to his wife, leaned in and asked, "Who wrote that?"

"My mother made that song, Lord Most High Emperor Husband."

"But why four? There are just three sisters—Thelma, Thia, and you, my beloved Thekla."

"There was a boy once, a brother ... then he was no more."

And though the ride was more somber after the song, a young husband held his wife more closely than ever before as the four rode back to the the few remaining fires kept burning in their stately home.

[11]

EDNA TELLS ALL

Children in the rafters
Babies on the floors
Toddlers on my apron strings
In and out of doors
See a need and meet it
Again again again
If they'd but give an hour's sleep
I might call them friends

Overcome with her own thoughts and emotions, Hilda did not notice the lack of applause this time around. Having finished the story and given her heart to the song, she sat, eyes closed, savoring. Memory, campfire glow, and evening breeze made up for the unchosen company.

Hot breath on her face brought her to her senses. Opening her eyes, she stared nose to snout with Jolene. The dragon's eyes were all flame.

"I do *not* feel happy. That story started happily and ended miserably," growled Jolene. The timber of Jolene's rumbling ire resonated long and low in Hilda's chest (who described the sensation later as the inverse of a cat's purr—times ten).

The maiden felt both shoulders gripped by claws barely sheathed.

"Sit, sister!" ordered Loretta.

Jolene did not budge.

Loretta crossed over and grasped her sibling by the forearm, pulling with all her sinewy strength, and returned Jolene one slow step at a time back to her seat. Wynona, watching unmoved, turned to their hostess and explained, "She doesn't do emotional long-suffering. Actually, none of us do. But Jolene is acutely allergic, always takes it personally."

Jolene stared across the fire, rocking herself and muttering, "make it happy make it happy make it happy make it happy make it happy." Her eyes were aflame, never leaving Hilda, never blinking.

Hilda sensed that it would be best for the next story to be light. Who knew the effects of pathos on dragons? A funny story came to mind, but she wondered if her three listeners would find it as humorous as the men in her clan.

"Would it be okay," Hilda asked, after drawing several deep breaths, "if the next story begins sad and ends happy?"

"Start and find out," grunted Loretta.

ONCE UPON A TIME, *on the outskirts of a village, just where the oxen were turned out to pasture, and the pigs roamed about burrowing with their noses among the roots of the trees, stood a small house. In the house lived a man named Simon who had an inconsolable wife.*

"Dear wife," Simon often said, "Why must you go about like a drooping rosebud? You have everything a husband can give a

wife. Why cannot you be merry like other women? Why do you not eat? And why is your heart grieved?"

"Leave me alone," his wife, Edna, would always answer through tears. "If I were to tell you, you would become just as wretched as I am. It is far better for you to know nothing."

Day after day, year after year, the husband would inquire about his wife's sadness, only to get the same reply.

One day, Simon decided to outwit and exhaust Edna by listing instances of good fortune. "Your cow is the best milker in all the village." he said. "Our trees are full of fruit and our hives are full of bees, yes? No one's cornfields grow straighter and taller than ours, correct?"

With each instance, Edna nodded. With each of her husband's listings, her head bobbled up and down and big tears fell upon their hardwood floor.

Simon stood defeated, crossed the space between them, and placed a tentative right arm around his wife's shoulder as she trembled. Then, quite against his will, a tear welled up in Simon's left eye. He wiped it away, hoping his wife did not notice.

"Yes, all that you say is true," Edna sputtered, "but ... (sniff) we have (snort) ... no children."

Then Simon understood. His eyes were opened and he could no longer be cheery. Starting that day, the little house on the outskirts contained a man whose unhappiness matched the sorrow of his wife.

At the sight of her husband's misery, Edna became more wretched than ever.

Some weeks passed and Simon grew desperate enough to seek outside consultation. He had heard of a wise man who lived eastward over the hills and took leave without saying much at all.

Simon had expected a long journey, but before evening he

found the man he sought sitting on a front porch, pipe in hand. Simon was overcome. Not realizing before that moment how deep was his desperation, he felt himself sink to his knees. He began to beg, "Give me children, lord wise man, give me children."

"Take care what you are asking," replied the wise man, unflustered. "Will not children be a burden to you? Are you rich enough to feed and clothe them?"

"Give them to me, my lord, and I will manage somehow!"

A moment later, Simon had a sign and blessing from the wise man and was sent on his way.

SIMON REACHED HOME *that evening tired and dusty, but with hope in his heart. As he drew near his house, the sound of young voices struck his ear. He looked up to see the whole place full of little ones: children in the garden, children in the yard, children looking out of every window. It seemed to Simon as if all the children in the world must be gathered before him. None seemed bigger than the next, all seemed terribly small, and each one was more noisy, more impudent, and more daring than the next. Simon gazed and grew cold with horror as he realized that they all now belonged to him.*

"Good gracious! How many there are!" he muttered to himself.

"Oh, but not one too many," said his wife smiling, coming up with a crowd of little ones clinging to her skirts.

By the next day though, even Edna found that it was not so easy to look after the three dozen plus four that had magically appeared calling her Mama, and Simon Daddy. Children were in the garden, the sitting room, the kitchen, and even roamed in and out of the now half-empty pantry.

By the second day, the children had eaten all the stored-up food and had begun to cry, "Daddy! I am hungry—I am hungry."

Simon scratched his head and wondered what he was to do next. In a single day he had found his life over-brimming with the joy of fatherhood, but now came a crisis. He did not know how he was to feed them. The cow was drying up, and it would be weeks before the fruit trees would ripen.

Simon turned to Edna and announced, "I must go out into the world and bring back food somehow."

The road to finding a way to feed three dozen plus four hungry children is long. It is made even longer when a man himself travels on an empty belly.

"This is not happiness!" complained Jolene, "just an impossible quandary. Would it not make more sense for the man and wife to eat a few, culling the brood down to more manageable size?"

"Hush, idiot," Wynona interrupted. "This is a peoples story, not a dragon one. Do you forget why we are here? Do I have to spell it out in front of ..." Wynona's eyes shot a sideways glance towards the girl-human.

Suddenly each dragon hushed, straightened, strained, and sniffed the wind then cocked their heads. All three, on point, listened in high-strung expectation.

"Let us be found doing our duty when she arrives," whispered Loretta.

Wynona nodded and motioned for Hilda to go on.

[12]

SIMON SETS OUT

Who are you?
so sad and tired
As soon as courage is required
Who are you?
though growing old
To do exactly as you're told

Simon wandered far and wide. At last, he reached a place so close to the end of the world that that which is mingles with that which is not. In the foreground he saw a sheepfold with seven sheep. Dozens more grazed in a field in the distance. In between stood a shepherd's hut. The idea entered Simon's mind that perhaps a single sheep would not be missed among so many ... that one small insignificant sheep would make a fine meal for his hungry family. Then Simon thought better of turning to thievery, though his stomach rumbled in protest.

As he walked towards the hut, racking his brain as to what he might offer in trade, a rushing noise swept over the field and drowned out the grumbling of his belly. Through the air flew a dragon. As Simon stood still and stared, the beast dove down and took as prey one full grown ewe in each claw.

Just as Simon began to register that he was not seeing things, out came a shepherd from the hut flailing his arms and yelling, "Every night?! Every night?! A pox on you and all your horrendous reptilian clan!"

Jolene giggled. Hilda relaxed into the enjoyment of storytelling.

Simon thought perhaps that this was not the right location to get food for his family. The competition looked fierce. But the hunger of his children back home clung to him like a burr, so, to his own surprise, a question tumbled out of his mouth addressing the shepherd, "What will you give me if I rid you of that beast?"

The shepherd had a ready answer. He had dreamt so often in his long hours of isolation of a hero appearing that he had written a little poem as a ready response—

> **Rams, one in three,**
> **I will give to thee**
> **Ewes, one in two**
> **I will give to you.**

"It is a bargain," said Simon, though he did not know how (supposing he **did** come out of the battle as victor) he would ever be able to drive home so large a flock.

Simon was suddenly very tired. He was thankful the shepherd offered shelter and he would think of how best to fight a dragon later. Tomorrow, after all, was another day.

The lonely shepherd found the presence of Simon so encour-

aging that he presented his guest with wine and an entire block of well-aged cheese. Of this, Simon had but a small bite, for he could not enjoy a full belly knowing the cow at home had, by this time, run dry. His children most likely were crying.

SIMON SLEPT WELL, *but the next night, as the sun sank, so did his stomach. A horrible feeling overcame him. He was sorely tempted to give up and take the shortest road home. He half started, then remembered his children and turned back to the challenge.*

"It is he or I," said Simon to himself. He took up position on the edge of the flock.

As the sun began to set, the air was filled with a rushing noise.

*As he could think of nothing else to say, Simon called out, "**Stop!**" in his most commanding tone.*

*The dragon lowered himself to the ground and exclaimed, "Who are **you**, and where did you come from?"*

"I am Simon Oliver Bolovan, who eats rocks all night, and in the day feeds the flowers of the mountain with carrion! If you meddle with these sheep I will carve my initials on your back!"

The dragon (unused to having his pattern of fly-snatch-and-return interrupted) stood like a statue in the middle of the road. "You will have to fight me first of course," he said hesitantly. It had been decades since the dragon had reviewed the etiquette between dragons and challenging knights, and he was sure none of his half-remembered lessons had mentioned a Simon-Oliver-Rock-Eating-Bolovan.

*Simon noted the serpent's pause and upped his bravado, "I fight **you**!?" he bellowed. "Why, I could slay you with one* blow!" Simon went into the shepherd's hut and retrieved the uneaten cheese. He laid out a challenge, "Go and get a stone like this out of the river and let us test strength against strength!"

The dragon did as Simon bade him, and brought back a stone twice as big as a man's head.

"Can you squeeze buttermilk out of your stone?" asked Simon.

The dragon picked up his stone with one hand, and squeezed it until it fell into powder, but not one drop of buttermilk flowed from it. "Of course I can't! You idiot!" the beast roared. "Milk does not come from stones." As the dragon brushed the dust off his claws, he cast about to remember where buttermilk **did** come from. *I always hated school,* he thought, *and now I am paying the price. Mama always said ...*

"Well, watch and learn," shouted Simon, interrupting the dragon's ponderings. Then, without hesitation, Simon-Oliver-Rock-Eating-Bolovan pressed the block of cheese until buttermilk flowed through all ten of his fingers.

When the dragon saw the oozing yellow, he felt it was perhaps past time for him to return home. But Simon stood in his cowering path.

"We have an account to settle," Simon growled. "You owe hundreds of sheep to this field and a year's back pay to the shepherd." (Listening from within the hut, the shepherd teared up and smiled at Simon's thoughtfulness).

The poor dragon was too frightened to speak, lest Simon should slay him and bury him among the flowers in the mountain pastures. But, in remembering his mother, he found an ounce of courageous inspiration.

From a nearby tree, the dragon tore a great branch and, as if it had been a feather, whirled it round his head and flung it three hundred yards across the field. Over the shepherd's hut it sailed, landing with a thud and scattering a group of huddled sheep.

"Beat that if you can, rock-eater!" he taunted.

Simon sauntered to the spot where the branch lay. The dragon followed, a single step behind. Simon shuddered inside as he felt the great beast's breath upon his shoulder.

Together they arrived, and Simon stooped to feel the branch. A great fear threatened to overcome him, for he knew that he and all his children together could not lift that limb from the ground.

"What are you doing?" asked the dragon.

"I was thinking," answered Simon, "what a beautiful branch this is, and what a pity that it should cause your death."

"How do you mean ... my death?" asked the dragon.

Simon did not answer but stood and stared up into the night sky.

"Just throw it," huffed the dragon.

"I must wait until the moon gets out of my way."

"I don't understand."

"Do you not see that the moon hampers my trajectory? Before the limb pierces you through the heart, like an arrow into a bull's-eye, it will arc high and take down the moon."

At these words the dragon grew uncomfortable for a second time. Not only did he not like the idea of being pierced through, he loved the moon and could not hunt without her light.

"I'll tell you what," the great serpent said, after thinking a little. "Don't throw the limb at all. I concede."

"No, certainly not!" replied Simon. "We will wait until the moon sets."

Simon would not budge, but while he stared the dragon slunk away to the road where he spread his wings and took flight. Before he soared aloft, he mumbled a promise over his shoulder that he intended never to return.

"I bet he lives with his mother, or an old wench like Auntie Maximilla in the Tobit story!" Jolene puffed up with the glee of insight. "I bet his mama makes him bring her ewe's milk to keep her looking young."

Jolene glanced back and forth at her compatriots, clicking her claws together in delight. They stared back at her through narrow slits and furrowed brows. Both motioned for silence.

Hilda continued.

[13]

DRAGON À LA CARTE

Can you burn me down a village
Dragon boy? Dragon boy?
Can you scoop me up a maiden like no other?
I could if I'd a mind to
And if I were in the mood
But I am a young thing and must go ask my mother

Simon took the dragon's promise to the shepherd and reminded him of their agreement.

The shepherd was grateful, but was also having second thoughts. He did not want to let a valuable guardian like Simon slip away. The shepherd hemmed and hawed about the uselessness of a dragon's word while Simon frowned.

Wynona, Loretta, and Jolene frowned also.

The shepherd, noticing his newly-dug stock pond was dry, added a condition. "If the dragon is really under your control," he challenged, "if you truly have him cowed ... prove he is your servant by making him fill my pond with water from the nearby brook."

Simon opened his mouth to protest. The shepherd popped into it a bit of bread and fruit and showed him to his bed saying, "If the dragon does not return in three days time, I will send you on your way with all the livestock promised and a wagon to boot."

Simon was more than weary. He was thankful for the food and would think of how he would get a flock of sheep and a wagon home later. Tomorrow, after all, was another day.

Two nights later, as the shepherd feared, the dragon did return. The beast was hoping that Simon had left and the sheep fields were guarded by a lesser man, as they had been before. Instead he found Simon scratching in the earth near the brook with a little knife. The dragon's curiosity gripped him, and he landed nearby to ask, "Why on earth are you digging about?"

"The shepherd begged me," answered Simon, "to fill his stock pond, and I do not feel like hauling bucket after bucket like a servile water boy. In a minute more, I will have redirected the entire brook, and the job will be done."

Now the dragon did not like the idea of any of his beautiful waterways being redirected. He loved the streams and found his way by looking down upon their coursing eddies. By the waterways he tracked the wide land below as he flew mile after mile.

"I will fetch the water myself. Do not change the brook's course!" the dragon begged.

Simon stood up from his work and pondered in silence for a long minute before saying, "I will allow you the honor of this task on two conditions."

"Agreed. What are they?" sputtered the desperate lizard.

"One, you will never prey on this shepherd's field again and two, you yourself will pull a giant cart with my new flock aboard, wherever and for how long I direct you. When I am out on quest, I usually return with a dragon's head as a trophy. I

*would be shamed to return to my palace if I did not at least make
a show of having tamed one to the point of doing my bidding."*

"Most certainly!" agreed the dragon, relieved the terms were
simple. He had heard from his mother's bedtime stories about
demands of weaving straw into gold and other impossible feats.
Men could be quite unreasonable but Simon-Oliver-Rock-
Eating-Bolovan was not.

Minutes later, the pond was brimming. The dragon filled it
in three trips and three mouthfuls.

The shepherd could no longer delay or argue. Simon had
kept his end of the bargain twice over. Before them stood a
dragon self-hitched to the shepherd's largest wagon. What could
the sheepman do but fill it with the promised rams and ewes?

Hilda looked at her still and silent audience. She knew
them well now by shape and shadow, how often each one
blinked, how deeply each one sighed. During their visitation
her vigilance had never waned, and now she was all at once
very, very tired.

Hilda yawned, but before her lips came together again, she
was brought up short. A fourth shape was sitting in the circle, a
new shadow dancing in the flame. A great Zendino was poking
the fire with a long beech branch, listening to every word with
eager intent. Geraldine had slipped in unheralded. Hilda
gulped. There was nothing to do but proceed.

THE DRAGON, *the wagon, and Simon set forth.*

*Still a mile from their destination, Simon thought he heard
his children's voices. He did not wish the dragon to know where
he lived, but what could he say to get rid of the monster?*

Simon stopped in the road. The dragon, one step behind,

stopped as well. The sheep began to bleat and Simon said, "At this juncture, I do not know what to do."

The dragon was panting, for the sheep were a toilsome load. Simon continued, "I have a hundred children, and I am afraid they may do you harm. I will do my best to protect you."

A hundred children sired by Simon-Oliver-Rock-Eating-Bolovan! The dragon lay down in terror. "Please release me from my harness," he begged. "I will leave and never again be seen in the lands of men."

Simon began to undo the dragon's bonds, extracting from him oath upon oath which were sealed with threats of great vengeance should he ever return. Just as the last strap was unbuckled, Simon's children appeared on the road before them. They, who had had nothing to eat for days, came rushing towards the great serpent, waving knives in their right hands and forks in their left. They cried out with one voice—

> **"Yummy, yummy!**
> **Dragon for our tummies!**
> **Thank you, Daddy, take**
> **your rest**
> **Dragon giblets are the best!"**

At this dreadful sound and sight, the dragon took off in adrenaline-fueled flight. So terrifying was his imagined fate that he never dared to show his face in the world again—even on its edges where that which is mingles with that which is not.

Hilda stood and curtsied, and this time there was clapping. Geraldine even whistled before stating flatly, "I've heard that one. You tell it well."

"Miss Geraldine, I presume?" asked Hilda, acting the hostess with all the confidence she could muster.

Wynona, Loretta, and Jolene sat trembling, but to Hilda, four dragons seemed no more threatening than three—an innocent mistake.

"What a darling young human!" Geraldine said, glancing at her troop. "And so good at weaving a plot line!" Turning back to Hilda, she added, "Would you like to hear the dragon song that goes with Simon-Oliver-Rock-Eating Bolovan? I hear humans like to sing round a camp fire."

"Please," answered Hilda, glad to give the floor to someone else. She almost wished she hadn't, though, for Geraldine sang off key and some of the lyrics were quite bawdy—

> *Simon cleaves to barren wife*
> *Then for children risks his life*
> *Though of the odds he's*
> *   terrified*
> *His heart can do no other*
> *I doubt a man can love his*
> *   brood*
> *With half the heart that*
> *   women do*
> *Grateful babes are far and few*
> *That call out thanks to father*

There was more. But Hilda, sitting upright, sank into a deep sleep. The last lines she remembered hearing went something like—

> *Fetch ewe's milk to keep her*
> *   young,*
> *Living with mama is awfully*
> *   fun.*

Balls cut off one by one ...

Unlike Hilda, Wynona, Loretta, and Jolene dared not drift off. They sat in full attention as Geraldine crooned song after song, verse after chorus after verse, long into the lonely night.

14

NO STEPMOTHERS ALLOWED

In this chapter, rhymes appear
with persistency
This couplet serves to fill the space,
for consistency

Just before dawn, Jolene shook Hilda awake. "Get some food for yourself, dearie, and us some more tea. Geraldine wants to hear a story from the beginning. We told her the whole extent of your skills. There may be singing too!"

Hilda pulled herself up from where she had collapsed before the fire pit and stumbled to the cabin. Upon entering, she washed her face and stepped towards the stove. Her mother had stood here often. What would Mother have done? First, she would make coffee instead of tea. Next, the dragon guests would have to take it black, in regular cups. Mother never would have caved and catered to their dragoniness. They were, after all, visiting a people house.

Hilda decided the guests could very well wait until she tidied up and ate a proper hot breakfast.

She thought of assigning the interlopers the chore of gathering firewood. Why not? It would be nothing to them, and it was because of them the woodpile was shrinking. She turned to suggest that very thing, but one determined step across the threshold was as far as the idea ventured. The rising sun illumined the hulking mass of reptilian flesh, causing Hilda to shudder. She drew back and collapsed into her mother's place at the family table. "Breathe, Hilda. Pray. Settle your mind into your heart. Find your bearings." Mother's words became her own.

Stepping once again towards the stove, Hilda found that while she had not the courage to insist on help from enemies, she still possessed the wherewithal to help herself. Coffee was set to brew. Ingredients were pulled from cupboards. She would have her fill of cornbread before venturing forth to play hostess once more.

As Hilda puttered, the dragons without prompting minded the fire, using their natural talent to keep flames hot and high. All the lowest limbs of the surrounding trees were broken off and piled nearby. The guests did not seem to notice the wait, and Geraldine prompted them to sing as they busied themselves.

From inside, Hilda did not attempt to follow the lyrics. She was too awash with gratitude that Geraldine had made herself choirmaster, rather than soloist.

> ***Brett only loved the breast and***
> ***thighs***
> ***The neck and head he tossed***
> ***aside***
> ***The skin disdained, the feet***
> ***long gone***

***To breasts and thighs his heart
belonged***

Three-part dragon harmony had a strange charm, but Hilda focused on the comforts close at hand: steaming coffee and melting butter. Her distractedness was for the best, for the words were troublingly insightful into the human condition—

> ***Gail fell in love with shirts
>   and ties
> The outline of a chosen man
> Enamored by the diamond ring
> Gleaming on her hand.
> Brett choked last night on boney
>   shard
> Gail's honeymoon, an
>   empty thud
> Dirty laundry in the yard
> Flinging rocks and mud***

Hilda waited until the song ended before exiting the cabin with a tray. She served four cups of black brew and sat, offering neither cream nor sugar. The dragons, so focused on handling the delicate stoneware, gave no notice of the contents. They sipped, gulped, stared at their hostess hungrily.

"There is a bit of leftover cornbread ..." Hilda offered.

Geraldine waved her off saying, "I hope I'm in time to sup on something besides leftover stories."

Hilda wiped her hands in her apron, wedged the empty tea tray between the stones she sat upon, and spread her arms. "I welcome requests. What kind of story would you like?"

Geraldine folded her limbs across her breast. "I am as old as these three combined," she declared, nodding towards the underlings, "so no moralizing plots. Give me something to sink my fangs into, like intricate motivations of more than one woman. And no stepmothers. Deliver me from the hoary cliche of stepmothers."

Hilda rubbed her forehead. Neither Jolene nor Wynona was going to speak up for her youth and innocence now. In fact, she wondered if any of the original three were going to speak again at all.

She had survived a single night in the company of dragons and had aged a decade in those dark hours. Perhaps a dark story would be fitting.

ONCE UPON A TIME *there were three royal brothers, Hubert, Dewey, and Lewis. Their parents had passed away and they lived in a great manor house together with their young stepsister Lantana. The brothers loved to hunt and their sister, who hated being left behind, followed them every time they went out tracking in the woods.*

Early one morning, the three princes (with Lantana tagging along of course) were closing in on a she-wolf creeping her way through the thick underbrush. Hubert drew back his bow, but just before he released the arrow, all three brothers had the shock of their young lives. The wolf spoke. "Do not shoot me! Do not shoot!" she cried, "for I have pups. If you spare me, I will give each of you one of my offspring and all will prove to be faithful friends."

Hubert did not argue. Who would want to shoot a talking wolf? As the group turned and walked away, they found that three little wolves followed, one after each brother.

Near noon, the hunting party approached a lioness saun-

tering among the brambles. Dewey drew back his bow and just before he released the arrow, all three brothers were surprised to hear the lion speak. "Do not shoot me! Do not shoot!" she cried. "For I have cubs. If you spare me I will give each of you one of my offspring and they will prove to be faithful friends."

Dewey did not argue. Who would want to shoot a talking lion? As they walked away, a little cub followed each of the brothers.

Towards evening, the three brothers drew near to a she-bear ambling her way between saplings. Lewis drew back his bow, but just before he released the arrow, none of the siblings were at all surprised to hear the mama bear speak. "Do not shoot me! Do not shoot!" she cried. "For I have cubs. If you spare me I will give each of you one of my offspring and they will prove to be faithful friends."

Lewis did not argue. Who would want to shoot a talking bear? The group walked away again, now with nine animals padding along behind, three after each brother.

Though it had been the most fascinating hunt of their young lives, Hubert, Dewey, and Lewis were all still itching to fire an arrow. Just before the sun began to set, they came to a clearing in the wood. Three birch trees grew at the juncture of three roads. Three brothers, three trees, three roads, and three of each kind of animal, seemed to them an ominous omen, full of meaning.

"Each of you shoot an arrow into a tree!" exclaimed Lantana, "and I shall read the signs."

Hubert, Dewey, and Lewis shrugged at the odd excitement of their sister as each one shot a single arrow into a birch tree.

While the arrows, stuck fast, were still reverberating, Lantana began to walk in a cloverleaf pattern round the trunks. She called for the animals to follow in her train, but none would leave the side of its new master. She pretended indifference and began to sing—

> *Arrows piercing birch*
> *wood deep*
> *Wait and watch, each wound*
> *will weep*
> *Blood from bark means*
> *archer's dead*
> *Milk means nothing yet to*
> *dread*

"Goodness, Lantana," said Dewey. "Must you always be so dark and disturbed?"

"I wasn't finished," said Lantana.

"At least sing in a major key," chided Lewis.

"Everybody dies," said Lantana. "The wolf, the lion, and the bear all know it. Why should we lie to ourselves? Anyway, if you had let me continue, you would have heard the next verse which says you all must pick a path—a separate path."

"Go ahead and sing the blasted thing," said Hubert. He was ready to move on, for the sun was getting low.

> *Bid goodbye and part your ways*
> *Come again in forty days*
> *How, in his quest, each one*
> *fares*
> *Will tell which man is Father's*
> *heir*

Hubert, Dewey, and Lewis conferred. They saw the wisdom of their sister's words. They knew there was a kingdom to rule, yet each one felt the other two more able. Something had to decide the kingship—staring at their accompanying beasts, there was no denying a change was brewing. Three little-traveled roads converging in the woods, three talking animals; these were undeniable harbingers that not even Lewis, the least mystical of the three, could deny.

Lantana, who was used to being left out of conferences and decisions, was surprised when her brothers turned and asked, "Sister, with which one of us do you wish to travel? Choose and tell the others goodbye, for in this wide, wild world, we may never see each other again."

Lantana had already chosen. "I will go with Hubert."

The brothers embraced and separated. They each set out upon a different road, followed by their beasts.

15

HUBERT TAKES THE CASTLE

I'm scented by a great grey wolf
Who watches me throughout the night
This news would cause me great alarm
Except a lion's at my side
The lion too might swallow me
While I sleep sound and unaware
But be assured I rest at ease
Protected by my bear

Hilda paused, wondering from what quarter commentary might come, yet knowing that now there was only one real source of feedback. Geraldine lip curled below her right nostril and Hilda, though now familiar with dragon facial contortions, could not tell if it was a smile or a sneer.

The elder dragon spoke. "So far, so good. Lantana has spunk ... refuses to be left behind. There might be a lesson for you in that, little human, eh? Must be hard to be left alone in the cabin with the menfolk gone." Hilda did not answer, but stared back unblinking.

Geraldine continued, "The brothers have, to a large degree, dominated their sister's choices. But that era is ending. I am intrigued. You may continue, but enough with the talking animals."

"Yes. Ma'am," answered Hilda, glad the voices of the lion, the wolf, and the bear were no longer crucial to the plot. Placing the empty coffee cups near the tray, she pressed on.

Lantana and Hubert traveled a day and a half along their chosen road. At night they slept soundly, curled in the arms of the bear and the lion while the wolf kept watch. At noon on the second day, they came to a wide glade in the center of which stood a gleaming castle. Hubert bade his animals and sister stay tucked within the woods while he approached and knocked.

The door opened, but instead of being invited in, four rough fellows came out and began to beat Hubert and strip him of his belongings. The attack came without warning. Hubert had no chance to pull his knife or cry out before he found himself face down in the dirt.

The ruffians paused to let him come to his feet, and laughed when he lifted his fists. But Hubert had no need to strike, for out from the woods came his beasts. Each animal, in a flash, had a man by the throat. Hubert took the fourth, dragged him inside, and threw him down into the root cellar with such force that the man lay as one dead.

When Hubert exited the castle, there was neither wounded man nor protective animal in sight. He called for Lantana to emerge from the woods. When he asked for a report of what she had witnessed, she said she had seen nothing, having buried her face in her hands when the violence began.

Lantana took Hubert's arm and they entered the castle together as the sun was beginning to set. There were many large rooms and a fine kitchen, but the place was ill-used and in need of much straightening and scrubbing.

"Brigands are horrible housekeepers," muttered Hubert, "but we will make a go of it. It seems at least all the windows are intact and the doors swing free."

The next morning, Hubert listed out for Lantana the work to be done. He told her that while she cleaned and swept and inventoried the remaining provisions, he would go out to hunt. Perhaps he could find what had happened to his beasts.

"Shall I send the bear back to you if I find him, sister?" he asked. "Though I don't think the man in the cellar will give you trouble since he is most likely dead."

Lantana spit out the bread she had been chewing in a sudden guffaw. Her brother smiled and added, "In any case, he is securely locked in. I'll decide what to do with him tomorrow."

"Don't bother about the bear, brother," Lantana replied. "If you send him, he will not stay. The animals belong to and obey you. Me, they simply tolerate."

Hubert shrugged and said, "You have a great deal to tackle. I hope you can manage without me, but it will be winter soon and I need to replenish what is left of the stores."

"Go ... go," said Lantana. "I am not a little girl."

LANTANA WANDERED all through the castle rooms noting unlit chimneys, broken bottles, filthy tapestries, and several ornamental settings with missing gems. I wonder, she thought to herself, where brigands hide jewels. I'll bet they bury them. So down Lantana went, her pace quickening, straight to the cellar door. Herbert had left the keys hanging in the kitchen and these she grabbed along with a large copper scoop to use for digging. If the jewels are not in the cellar, she mused, then I'll ladle up the whole garden.

Lantana opened the cellar door and stepped over the body of

the fourth bandit. Lighting a lamp, she peered down the long and dusty corridor before trodding forward, poking and prodding the musty interior. Though she found several bottles of well-aged wine, Lantana did not see a single jewel nor any sign of freshly dug hiding places.

On her way out, she was pleased to find an iron spade. Dropping the copper ladle in excitement, she decided after lunch she would upend the garden. She was so focused on her plans she did not notice there was no body to step over as she exited. Spade and keys in hand, she turned and relocked the cellar door.

Lantana hummed to herself as she wandered towards the pantry. She hoped there was more day-old bread in one of the cupboards. For though she knew how to cook and had been taught how to clean, she had no intention of doing either. When she arrived in the kitchen, she dropped the spade in shock. There before her was a table set with fine china, wine, grapes, and cheese. And, turning from the stove with spoon in hand was the brigand. Rugged manliness was not diminished by the donning of a well-starched apron, any more than rough-cut winsomeness could be hidden by his one black eye.

"Madam, I am Morris," said the stranger bowing low. "I had hoped to cook for your brother as well, to make up for my earlier bad manners. But to be honest, it is nice to speak to you alone."

Lantana said nothing and stepped towards the table.

[16]

DEWEY BY THE SEA

A dragon a dragon
I swear I saw a dragon
Three-headed monster
quite the beast
Three minds made up
to on me feast

Dewey, the second eldest prince, set out on his adventure alone. He traveled a day and a half along his chosen road, sleeping soundly curled in the arms of the wolf, while the bear and lion kept watch.

"But ... but what about Lantana and Morris!" cried out Jolene like one pained. "Why did you leave that thread of the story?! I don't care about Dewey!" Jolene stamped her back feet in frustration.

Geraldine spat in the fire and glared. Jolene looked up and whimpered.

"Can you say 'cliffhanger,' Jolene?" Geraldine sneered with edged sarcasm.

"Cliffhanger."

"And," continued the dragon matriarch, "Since I know you cannot define it, perhaps your sister will for you."

Loretta sat up very straight, pressing her fist to her forehead, but no words came.

"Wynona, my pet?" oozed Geraldine, "Would you like to save your classmates once more?"

"Cliffhanger, noun," said Wynona, "a melodramatic or adventure story in which each section ends in high suspense in order to keep a listener's interest. Example in human lore: 'The knight hung on the edge of the cliff as the dragon circled above.' Cliffhanger."

"Who cares about knights?" pouted Jolene.

"Humans do," answered Geraldine, "and unless you wish to be dinner, I expect not another word from your wanna-happy-ending snout."

Jolene nodded. Her shoulders sank, her lower lip jutted out.

"Would you like me to continue?" asked Hilda.

Geraldine bowed. "Pardon Jolene's youth. She will not speak again, and if she does, she will not speak *ever* again."

AT NOON THE SECOND DAY, Dewey came to an inn. Leaving his companions in the woods, he entered and spent a coin on food and drink.

Everyone in the inn seemed distressed, so Dewey inquired of those who dined nearby what was the matter. They grunted but told him nothing. After eating, Dewey put his question to the proprietor.

"Ah," replied the innkeeper, "today our lord's daughter is to die, handed over as tribute to a dreadful three-headed dragon."

Dewey looked aghast.

"Don't judge us son," said the bartender. "The dragon will burn down the town if he is not given his due, and the lord of the manor has grown old. Besides, this is his fifth daughter, who he had hoped would be the first of sons."

Dewey thought the death of a beautiful maiden, even fifth-born, was a waste. Knowing himself to be strong, young, and able, he inquired where the exchange with the dragon was to take place. (He was careful to keep his indignation in check.) The half-drunk patrons all pointed in the same direction and answered in chorus, "At the shore, by the sea ..."

As Dewey departed, he heard them continue a drinking song prompted by his request for directions—

> **At the shore**
> **By the sea**
> **By the beautiful sea**
> **Dragon takes**
> **In the waves**
> **My lady from me**

"I will save her," Dewey muttered, "or die trying." And he set out to the seashore, followed by his three beasts.

As Prince Dewey went towards the sea, a great company of people were traveling the same path in the opposite direction. Seeing his bear, wolf, and lion, they gave him wide berth, but Dewey could see on their faces a great sadness. He learned from snatches of their conversations that this was the crowd that had accompanied the princess to her doom.

When Dewey arrived at the shore, he saw a lone maiden bound tight, doing her best to look brave. He also saw, out in the waves a long way off, movement skimming along the tops of the *foaming breakers. Across the waters was coming a terrible dragon with three long necks. A grotesque head sat upon each.*

The prince, unflinching, took counsel with his beasts.

Bear, wolf, and lion lined up between the damsel and the shoreline, facing the waves. Each dragon neck stretched towards a waiting foe as the gap closed. It would be a great battle—three against three. The damsel, now overwhelmed, fainted dead away. If the dragon won, she was bride to a monster. If he lost, she would be devoured by one of the creatures of the forest. She had not the energy or wherewithal to notice Dewey.

The dragon took no notice of Dewey either, and this suited the prince well. Dewey crouched low and drew his bow, planting one foot in the waves and taking aim perpendicular to the shoreline. The dragon, furious that three beasts stood between himself and the rights due him, paid no mind to his flank. Three necks jutted forward in a triple-synchronized lunge, aiming to plunge teeth into the necks of waiting bear, wolf, and lion. Just as the three heads aligned, an arrow flew. Sharp tip and straight shaft wove through the first head's eye sockets, pierced the second mouth's tongue, and lodged the entirety of the projectile into the ear canal of the third cranium. Searing pain, blindness, dumbness, and deafness followed. Bear, wolf, and lion rushed forward and tore the dragon's body into a thousand pieces.

Hilda wanted no commentary but was sure, at this juncture, it would come. A moment's hesitation was met with silence. She breathed but once, and resumed.

WHILE THREE BEASTS supped on dragon, Prince Dewey inspected the unconscious damsel. He could tell from the crest on her handkerchief and signet ring that she was from the royal line of Lagobel. It was to that land she needed to return.

She was lovely to behold but not slight in form. Prince Dewey did not know how far he could carry her, and did not think it prudent to harness any of his creatures to pull a stretcher. Besides, it seemed each of them had taken a portion of the carcass to the forest to eat in private. They were nowhere in sight.

Great was Dewey's relief to see a late-coming coach roll up, tardy for the earlier festivities that bid Her Highness adieu. Dewey approached the coachman, explaining all that had transpired, keeping to himself the coordinated effort between man and beasts.

"Climb into the carriage with the damsel," offered the coachman. "I will pass near her father's palace before I cross back over the mountains. Perhaps she will awaken in your arms."

Dewey was relieved, and pulled the sleeping maiden in upon the velvet cushions awaiting them. He sighed at his good fortune and hoped the rescued lady would regain her wits before they had traveled far.

But the coach was not traveling towards Lagobel. It belonged to the damsel's enemies. Hours later, Dewey found himself, bound and gaged, tumbling down the face of a ravine.

LEWIS BY THE FIRE

What happens next?
What happens next?
You leave your audience perplexed
How should I know?
How should I know?
The tale is woven as I go

Prince Lewis took the third path, followed by his faithful beasts.

Geraldine mouthed "cliffhanger" and the other three copied her silent enunciation. Jolene, in particular, was careful that she made not a sound.

Darkness came on, and Lewis curled up in the arms of the lion, as the bear and wolf kept watch. The next morning, halfway to noon, the path came to a dead end. Not wanting to turn back and wander in the same direction as his brothers, Lewis pressed forward as best he could through the underbrush. Hour after hour he fought his way through the brambles, growing more bewildered as the day wore on. The beasts followed doggedly at his disoriented steps as he forged a path into the looming darkness. Then his heart was infused with hope, for the light of a fire leapt up from the shadows ahead.

As Lewis drew near the light, he spied an old woman raking sticks and dried leaves together and burning them in an oblong glade. The prince was weary, darkness was seeping in, so he called out for permission to spend the night beside the old woman's fire.

"Of course you may, young prince," she answered, "but I am afraid of your beasts."

Lewis turned to see. The bear, the lion, and the wolf stood in the shadow cast behind him, and all looked fierce. "They are quite tame. Come see, mother." He bade his lion, and wolf, and bear to lay down and roll over, bellies up. Reluctantly, they obeyed.

The old woman crept up and hid behind Lewis, peeking round him to see the animals were subdued. With a sudden leap forward she pulled forth a rod and struck each of them. One after the other—lion, and wolf, and bear—they turned to stone.

Prince Lewis stood in shock. Then the old woman, with a gleeful cackle, brought her rod down upon him as well.

Hilda paused. Wynona and Loretta mouthed "cliffhanger." Jolene yipped with shrill excitement, "Back to Morris and Lantana! What happens!? What happens!?"

Geraldine stood up and crossed over to Jolene. Taking her head into head in her hands, she unceremoniously snapped her neck. Jolene slumped backward and Geraldine returned to her seat before the fire.

"Shall I continue?" said Hilda in a shocked and barely audible voice. The words came only by habit.

"No!" ordered Geraldine. "I've heard enough: three species, three brothers, three women. Trope. Trope. Trope. First, the stepsister must attach herself to a man, a good-brother then a rogue. Classic pretty young female chooses bad boy. Overdone. The second female spends her time unconscious, a helpless victim tied to the stake until plopped down to loll about on velvet carriage cushions. The third female is an old witchy woman in the woods. Nothing new to see here."

Wynona and Loretta sat, mouths open.

Hilda stared at the lifeless Jolene. Would her carcass be dinner for her monstrous companions, or did dragons ever speak in hyperbole?

Loretta raised a hand.

"You may speak, Loretta."

"So no more story ... we're stuck not knowing?"

"Yes. Knowing is useless unless you are learning," growled Geraldine.

Loretta, glancing sideways at her very still sister, decided she had no more questions.

"Wynona," Geraldine called out, "Please wrap up the plot for Loretta."

"Well, from the human stories I have heard before," said Wynona with no little arrogance, "I would guess that Morris seduces Lantana and she likes it until she doesn't. Next, Dewey's beasts will help him rescue both his brothers, and he will marry the unconscious princess. I'll bet he has her handkerchief tucked away somewhere as proof of his valor."

Geraldine nodded in half-hidden pride. At least one of her students was progressing.

Loretta blurted, "But ..." then stifled her own mouth.

"Go ahead, Loretta. I don't feel up to killing twice in one day. Jolene will provide plenty for all."

"But," Loretta said, "Dewey is middle-born. Middle-borns never get to marry the princess. I ... I thought that was a rule."

"Good eye! Good ear! Good nose for human plots!"

congratulated Geraldine, "but think ... why, in this tale, is there an exception?"

Loretta drummed her forehead with her claws.

"How about you tell us, Hilda?" said Geraldine, swinging round.

"Because he killed the dragon," replied Hilda without hesitation. She saw no harm in stating the obvious and no use in playing dumb.

"Exactly!" puffed the matriarch. "Take this lesson, ladies— a man could be covered in pimples, balding, a fool, produce constant flatulence, and own no more than a belt round his naked waist. But if he kills the dragon in these pathetic people tales, a beautiful, rich, high-achieving, talented, brilliant princess will take him to her bed to produce brat after brat with him."

Wynona and Loretta sat silent.

"Do you know why?" asked Geraldine.

Wynona and Loretta shook their heads.

"Do *you* know why, human? Could you provide some values clarification?"

Hilda shook her head.

"Because," crowed Geraldine, "we dragons are wrapped round the human brain stem. Never forget this, my pupils, and I guarantee you will never become imbedded in one of humanity's over-wrought, over-hyped, over-told tales. We are the basis of all human fears."

[18]

SPACE TO BREATHE

Dragons in the rafters
Dragons on the floors
Dragons round my campfire
Just outside my door
Dragon soot on windows
Useless are my locks
Dragon drool and drivel
Splattered on my frock

Geraldine excused Hilda to the cabin while the dragons dined. "It's for your own good," she said. "Don't want to traumatize you any more than we already have." Hilda could hear the crunching and slurping even when pressed against the back interior wall.

When would the men come back? She wondered. Worn down, no longer able to stoke up courage, Hilda felt creeping despair under Geraldine's watchful eyes and critical ears. Should she feel better that now there were only three guests? No comfort came. And there was something tragic about the loss of Jolene, though Hilda had not forgotten her flaming eyes and tightening grip. A ring of bruises on each of Hilda's upper arm testified to the terrible confrontation.

Knowing she had space to breathe until evening, when the next round of entertainment was slotted, Hilda slipped out a back window with a basket for berry picking. She would not be looked for again until the sun began to set. After eating, the dragons would sleep.

Hilda felt her feet wander further and further. Down she went to her old childhood haunt near the streambed. The flow and laugh of the running water calmed her trembling heart and filled her ears with clean pleasantness. If the weather had been warmer, she would have stripped off her dress (spattered with dragon tea and coffee and dribbled with dragon drool and sweat) and plunged in. Even her hair smelled like dragon, and she wanted to wash it away along with every evil she had lately been forced to reckon with.

There was no use running. No one outran dragons. They had to lose interest and this pack was still spellbound. Where was the border between telling a tale too well and telling it too poorly? How did one spin a yarn aptly enough to be valuable alive, but not so mesmerizingly that the audience asked for another, and another, and yet another? She had fulfilled the storytelling task at the highest caliber, and was paying the price for her excellence.

Hilda stared at her tired face in the shallow current. She felt hungry now, but her basket was empty.

Another reflection came up, peering over her shoulder. It was Oran's.

Up Hilda leapt with a cry. Older brother had come home, he would know what to do. She splashed across the stream and was at once in his arms.

"It is nice that you come out and greet me, sister," laughed

Oran, "but I was rather hoping you would be at the stove stirring something hot. I am famished."

"It is providence you did not get so far, brother," replied Hilda, "for we have guests."

Something in her tone told Oran, and then there was her smell.

"Dragons in the cabin?"

"Well, just outside it ..."

"How many?" Oran asked.

"Do I count the dead?"

Oran raised an eyebrow.

"Three ... very much alive, feeding on one."

The siblings sat on the shore together as Hilda continued, "Two Rekikis and one Sarkani—an adolescent thank God— showed up two days ago. A Zendino joined them in the middle of last night. I am worn out."

Oran gazed at his little sister with a look she had not seen before. Hilda filled her lungs and let out a deep breath, "You smell of dragon too, brother."

"I have been with father, crossing wits with a single Zendino," answered Oran. "You have, in the meantime, been discoursing with three, a Sarkani among them. How in the world have you managed?"

"I served them tea and coffee and told them stories."

"Tea and stories ..."

Hilda said, "And you and Father have been trapped by a Zendino ... your tardiness makes sense now, but Oran, I could use a spotter. You weave fantastic tales ... I feel ready to collapse. It's not just entertainment. I'm the subject of an experiment or an observed animal. One mistake, and I will become an hors d'oeuvre."

"*That* is an accurate assessment, sister, and until they are satisfied, there is not much I can do. A man might tell half a story before he is eaten. How many tales have you made it through?"

"Three … and a half."

Oran gave a low whistle. "No wonder you're exhausted."

Hilda nodded and sighed. She shuddered realizing three and a half was also the current head count in front of the cabin.

Oran took his sister into his arms. "Hilda, you've done amazingly and you are stronger than either of us thought. I would have been dead before I reached a single plot twist."

Hilda squeezed him back and begged, "Can't you at least stay in the shadows, unseen?"

"Perhaps for a bit," Oran said, "but I will be wanted back. Father and I and our one dragon have a kind of short-term truce. The great Zendino says she will return to the lake in the morning with an answer to Father's riddle. I've just come to recuperate for a spell, and grab provisions and ale. Father has not taken well to drinking lake water."

"How long do these trials, these negations, go on?" said Hilda, not expecting an answer.

"Ours will end by tomorrow," replied Oran, "for Geraldine has given us her word. If she cannot answer the riddle before tomorrow's sunset, she will never show her face in Lagobel again."

"Her name is Geraldine?"

"Yes."

"That's *my* Zendino. The one eating a Rekiki right now in front of the cabin."

Oran paused and thought as this piece of fascinating information was sorted and put in its place.

"She's heard your stories," he said at last. "Does she know your station?"

"I am a youngling, a simple country maiden to my guests. They order me about and I do not protest. They have no interest in personal history. They crave sagas, lore, stories of 'the peoples.'"

"Research ... she's doing research," Oran mused aloud. "She supposes the more she knows of humans, the better her chances of answering Father's riddle. How blessed we are that she has not guessed that she has Kenterick kin in her clutches."

"Should you tell me the riddle, so I won't betray you and father through ignorance?" asked Hilda.

Oran thought for some time, paced several strides back and forth along the bank, then answered, "No. Knowing would change your tone, your posture, your simplicity."

"But what if I give something away? What if she guesses my connections?"

Oran pulled at his beard. "Do you know 'The Ring and the Drow-Maiden'?"

Hilda nodded.

"Tell your guests that one. It will infuriate Geraldine but it will bring her no closer."

"An infuriated Zendino on my hands," said Hilda. "Thanks."

"Hopefully," quipped Oran, "it doesn't also piss off the Sarkani."

THE RING AND THE DROW-MAIDEN

Boris the dwarf spoke slowly to Gleb
Most of his words went over Gleb's head

That evening Hilda sat silent. The dragons waited. Hilda crossed her arms. Loretta twiddled her thumbs. Wynona did her best to mirror all the movements and gestures of Geraldine.

"What is it, youngling?" said Geraldine. "One more is not much to ask. Your break went long and our bellies are full. There is no danger of being eaten at present."

Hilda shook her head. "Not another 'once upon a time' until I have some assurances."

"Well, well ... finding your own mind and voice, are you?"

Geraldine turned towards Wynona. "This could get very educative. Pay close attention. What kind of assurances, human, do you wish for?"

Hilda did not hesitate. "One—when I say, 'The End,' it is not just the end of another story but the end of our acquaintance. You three leave and I stay, just as I am with my home intact. Two—take off the prohibition on either talking animals or stories with stepmothers. It leaves my options unbearably narrow."

"And if we refuse?"

"No story. I figure you'll eat me either way ... unless you promise." Hilda now twiddled her own thumbs in feigned casualness. "I have heard dragons are wary of breaking their word."

"Which is why we rarely give it," said Geraldine.

"Well, give me your word," shot back Hilda, "or shove me down your gullet now to join Jolene."

Geraldine stroked her beard, "You, little one, so young, barely from your egg ... already fighting and conniving. You could be one of us."

"I am human, ma'am, one of the peoples," said Hilda with ferocity. "We do not do as dragons do."

"Really ... ?" said Geraldine, picking up a stray bone to clean her teeth. "Are you sure?"

Hilda did not flinch. "Did you hear my conditions? Do you give your word?"

"Let me see. One—we must leave at 'The End,' with your property, life, and limbs intact. If you get to the end, then yes, you have my word. And two—talking animals or stepmothers ... which one ... hmm. You may have the animals."

"Your word."

"I, Geraldine of the Greater Zendino, give you my word."

Hilda rose, threw a log in the fire, and began.

The Sarkani, the great dragons of the north, are breathtaking to behold. They lay waste to whole tracts of country, devouring both men and beasts. Those who see them and survive say they have a body like an ox—but bigger times five—and hind legs like a bullfrog, not slimy but sinewy and spring-loaded, able to catapult the beast forward ten times its body length. The forearms, by comparison, are quite short. A third set of long appendages protrude just inside Sarkani shoulder blades, forming bat-like wings. The mighty tail grows with the dragon, always remaining twice as long as the beast to which it belongs.

Sarkani skin is an intricate network of interlocking scales, harder than stone. Its two great eyes pierce daylight and shine like searchlights by night. Anyone who looks into those great shining orbs becomes bewitched, rushing of his own accord into the monster's jaws.

Wynona stood up, unfurled her wings, and jutted out her long snout towards the sky. She was, even in her youth, a sight to behold. She held her pose for a long ten seconds, then folded her pinions, laced her clawed fingers, and sat to listen once more.

When a Sarkani appeared in the central kingdom of Endelion, ten years before the great earthquake, all animosity between jurisdictions disappeared. Neighboring kings forgot petty rivalries and formed cooperatives. Rulers pooled resources to offer rich incentives. Multiple king's daughters were set out as possible brides for any man able to destroy the monster, whether by force, trickery, or enchantment. One king who shall go unnamed offered two daughters, willing to wed both to one man.

Sarkani dragons, it was rumored, might be overcome by riddles, magic rings, or the promise of gold. Gleb of Glenbrook had none of these things. But the idea of a woodsman marrying a princess fascinated him. One of the king's daughters had caught his fancy. (One wife would be plenty for him. Gleb knew just enough to shudder at the idea of two.)

Daydreams of heroic deeds and young love was transformed to practical necessity when Gleb realized the beautiful woodland in which he lived was in danger. The dreaded beast was moving ever nearer. When a Sarkani takes possession, it moves on only after it scorches the earth down to bedrock, burning away not just trees and underbrush but the very topsoil. Gleb thought that possibly he might be at the beginning stages of love for a certain princess, but he knew he loved the trees. And, if the forest was turned to barren wilderness, he could not earn his bread. He was very certain of his need to eat.

A DWARF NAMED *Boris lived at the heart of Glenbrook Forest.*

At the word "dwarf" all three dragons, in chorus, humphed and rolled their eyes.

Boris had made a hand-carved home within the third-largest tree. He had little interest in princesses and even less in dragons. He had no need to earn his bread since he squirreled away nuts for sustenance, just enough and no more to keep his small body alive. But Boris loved the trees as much as Gleb. In this, they understood one another.

The dwarf was not unaware of the dragon's nearness, so he mentioned to the woodsman in passing that one might-perhaps-maybe discover the secret to killing a Sarkani dragon if one could gain the signet ring once possessed by the famed King Glockenspiel. Glockenspiel's ring was perhaps-maybe-possibly engraved with an inscription with instructions on how a brave man might-maybe vanquish the encroaching nemesis. Also, in a tiny script etched with a fairy needle, along the shining rim of the golden ring, a second inscription instructed how a coura-geous warrior might-perhaps-maybe survive.

Gleb thanked Boris, surprised not only that the tree-dwelling dwarf spoke a well-educated King's English, but that they shared the same burning concern. Hoping to continue the conversation, Gleb ventured a question, "Where do you think the ring is now?"

"I can only suggest a direction," answered Boris. "East. All wisdom worth knowing these days comes from the East."

"Could you elaborate a bit further?" said Gleb, keeping his

tone polite but firm. He had heard dwarfs would not converse with those who did not demand respect.

Boris sighed and said (more to himself than to Gleb), "There's nothing for it but to teach him bird."

"Bird?" said Gleb. "You want to give me a bird?"

"Their language," said Boris, now wishing he had not begun the conversation in the first place. "The birds of the air will guide you, if you learn to understand their chatter."

"I did not make good marks in school," said Gleb, now wishing he had not asked any further questions. "Languages, even my own native tongue, get all twisted when I make an effort to pin them down. I have often daydreamed," he continued, sighing (more to himself than to Boris), "of a rune, or a spell, or a potion that puts the knowledge inside me all at once."

"There is a way," muttered Boris. He wondered now if he would have a single trade secret left at the end of the interchange. He bade Gleb sit as he mixed a powerful brew of nine herbs gathered alone by moonlight. Of this he gave Gleb nine spoonfuls and ordered him to return for a second and third dose over the next three days.

After the last dosage, Gleb heard not another word from Boris except, "Go east, listen to the birds, and if you ever find Glockenspiel's ring come back to me. I may be able, by then, to perhaps-maybe explain the inscription to you."

"Both inscriptions," said Gleb, but Boris made no answer.

THE FIRST WEEK of Gleb's travel was tedious. He felt a meaningless aimlessness set in, as though very little, if any, progress were being made. He grew tired, and hot, and bored with walking.

The second week of Gleb's travel was monotonous. He felt

the meaningless aimlessness set in to his bones, like no progress at all was being made. He grew more tired, and hot, and bored with walking.

The third week of Gleb's travel felt counter-productive. He was overwhelmed by meaningless aimlessness, a sense of regression, and uprooted purposelessness. He was tired, and hot, and bored with walking.

At the beginning of the fourth week, Gleb, hot and tired and bored, sat down under a tree in a strange forest to eat his supper. After a few bites of dried bread, he noticed that two rose-breasted yellow-plumed silverbeaks sat above him. The birds looked down upon the human quizzically. One said to the other, "That is a wandering fool—a stultus errans."

Geraldine grunted but held her tongue. Hilda pretended not to notice.

"I believe you are right in your classification, my dear," said her mate. "He is far from his conclave and migrating erratically. I wonder if he, having come so far, will find what he is looking for."

The bird-wife was quick to answer, "He will have to seek help from the drow-maid. If she has not got what he wants herself, she will know well enough who has it."

"But where is he to find the drow-maiden?" said her husband. "He might as well try to catch the wind."

"Once a month she comes to a nearby spring to wash her face under the light of the full moon."

"That is in three days time," mused the husband-bird. "I never understood her ritualistic washing, and why once a month?"

"As to the interval," said the wife-bird, "I have not the energy to explain, but as for why she washes, she does so to never grow old. Coming to the spring keeps her wrinkle-free and in the bloom of her youth."

"We should fly to the spring," said the husband-bird, wink-ing. "Perhaps the stultus errans will follow."

"Yes! Yes!" chirped his wife and away they flew.

Gleb somehow tracked the rose-breasted yellow-plumed silverbeaks, though he often lost sight of them. The birds, for their part, enjoyed the novelty of being followed, but forgot more than once that the wandering fool had no wings to carry him along. They never noticed that Gleb's heart beat with anxiety lest he should lose sight of his guides.

At last, the birds reached a clearing in the forest and settled to roost at the top of a high tree. A clear spring bubbled in the middle of the green space below. Gleb sat down at the foot of the birds' chosen perch to watch and listen. The silverbeaks went on and on, chattering, not caring whether or not they were understood.

"When the drow-maiden comes to the spring, do you think, husband, that she will be dissuaded from bathing by the wandering fool? She is quite secretive you know."

"Nothing escapes her notice," said her spouse. "It will be a fascinating interaction. But I think the main question is whether or not the youth has the sense to not let himself get caught in her coils."

"Wait and see, wait and see," came the wifely answer.

THE MOON WAS SHINING down upon the forest when Gleb heard a slight rustling sound.

From the west side of the clearing, out of the forest came a maiden gliding over the grass. Her feet seemed scarcely to touch the ground.

Gleb could not turn away his eyes. He had never in his life

seen a woman so beautiful. None of the princesses from the kingly co-op could compare.

The drow-maiden drifted straight to the spring where she stood looking up to the full moon. She knelt down and bathed her face nine times, stood, and faced skyward again. She walked nine times round the spring and as she went, she sang—

> **Full-faced moon with light**
> **unshaded,**
> **Let my beauty ne'er be faded.**
> **Aged wrinkles now forbid!**
> **Though the moon is waning**
> **nightly,**
> **May my youth bloom always**
> **brightly,**
> **Gnarling greying ever hid.**

The maiden dried her face with her long hair, and was about to go back under the shelter of the trees when her eye caught sight of the youth watching slack-jawed. She crossed the green lawn towards him with ever quickening pace. Gleb stood up, waiting.

Her voice was stern and cutting. "You presumed to watch my secrets in the moonlight! Who are you? How have you come to this place?"

Gleb, somehow finding his voice, said, "Forgive me, beautiful maiden, for offending you. I chanced to come here after a long wandering and was resting under the tree. When you came, I did not know what to do, so I stayed where I was. I did not think that my watching would offend you. I see now I was wrong."

Hearing his answer, the tone of the drow-maiden changed.

"Come. It is better to rest upon a pillow than upon damp moss. You shall spend the night under my roof."

Gleb was amazed at this turn of events, but hesitated. The birds called from the top of the tree assuring him—

> **Go, go, she calls, she calls**
> **The ring, the ring, go go**
> **but give no blood**
> **no blood, no blood**
> **or she will have your soul.**

[20]

DRAGON FLAME

How can I believe you
Unless you show me?
My little darling,
Don't you know me?

The garden of the drow-maiden was magnificent to behold. Beyond the beautiful lawn stood a splendid house, glittering in the moonlight, gilded in gold and silver. When Gleb entered the palace he found many sumptuous chambers lit by hundreds of tapers burning in golden candlesticks.

At length, the maiden led him to a room where a feast was spread upon ornate silver dishes. His hostess seated herself in a golden chair, and offered a silver one to Gleb. They dined in silence, served by maids dressed in white.

Gleb felt overcome by the beauty of his surroundings, the aliveness of his taste buds, and the softness of their after-dinner conversation. The drow-maiden took his arm and led him though room after room until she herself tucked him into a silken bed under a downy comforter. The last words he heard her say before sinking into euphoric sleep were, "Would you not like to stay here always? I do not age, am very rich, and have no guardian. We can do as we like."

The next morning, while Gleb dressed for breakfast, the maiden herself brought him a tray. She wore a look that expected an answer.

Gleb took her hand with gentle caution saying, "Don't be angry, dear maiden. I do not decide in haste on any important matter. And what could possibly be more important than whether or not I remain with you?"

"But of course!" she breathed in rushed interruption. "Take weeks if you like to know your heart." She pressed Gleb's hand to her chest and added, "I am Gwyllion, my darling. I do not honor many with my true feelings, much less my name."

Gleb nodded and she left him to eat alone with his thoughts.

Gleb did not see Gwyllion again until dinner. He passed his time wandering the halls. The air felt thick with enchantment, but all five of his senses testified to the reality of wall, and rug, and tapestry. Gleb did not know what course of action to take, and was no closer to discerning it when he was summoned to dinner.

After another silent meal Gwyllion took Gleb to a secret chamber where a little gold box stood on a silver table. "Here is my greatest treasure," she said, "a precious gold ring which will be yours when ... I mean **if** ... you marry me." She smiled and her eyes shone bright.

"It is indeed beautiful," admitted Gleb.

"See the small stone in the center, how it glows?" Gwyllion went on. "Tradition says a groom, on his wedding eve, pricks the smallest finger on his left hand and wets the gem with a drop of his own blood. In doing this, the ring brings the wearer to heights of wedded bliss, and the couple's love lasts until death ... sometimes even beyond."

Gleb, determined to guard his soul, hid his feelings. He took the maiden's hand in his and said, "I am overwhelmed by even the thought of such a gift. Tell me more about this magical ring, for I struggle to believe it."

"No one fully understands," Gwyllion said, "because no one can read the secret signs engraved upon it. I'm told it once belonged to King Glockenspiel of Endelion, whoever he was. Still, even without knowledge of the runes, I can work great wonders with it."

"Show me, darling," breathed Gleb.

She said, "If I put the ring upon the little finger of my left hand—I can fly like a bird through the air, wherever I wish to go. If I put the ring upon the fourth finger of my left hand—I am invisible, and can see everything that passes round, though no one can see me. If I put the ring upon the middle finger of my left hand—neither fire nor water nor any sharp weapon can hurt me. If I put the ring upon the thumb of my left hand—that hand becomes so strong that it can break rocks and shatter walls."

Gleb stood dumbfounded as Gwyllion put the ring back into its box.

"My darling," said Gleb with an eyebrow upraised, "I want to believe all that you say, but it sounds like legend, like a bedtime story."

Gwyllion reopened the box.

"Perhaps," she said, "seeing is believing." The ring glittered like the clearest sunbeam as she held it out. The maiden put it on fourth finger of her left hand, and disappeared from sight.

"Do not tease me!" called out Gleb. "My heart aches, my love, when I do not see you!"

With that Gwyllion reappeared and smiled.

"It is my turn now," Gleb said with a wink.

And Gwyllion handed him the ring.

Gleb, without hesitation, put the ring on the little finger of his left hand, and soared into the air like a bird.

Gwyllion saw him fly and cried, "Come back down now, my love. My heart aches when you are not beside me. And now you see I have told you the truth."

Soaring ever higher, Gleb was gone.

GLEB DID NOT HALT or even slow until he reached the home of Boris. The dwarf was delighted to find that Gleb's search had been successful. The Sarkani dragon was drawing ever closer and both could smell the smoke.

Boris at once set to work interpreting the secret signs engraved upon the ring. There was no potion or herb to speed the learning this time, and it took him forty days' hard work to squeeze the meaning from the engraving. Three days more were required to interpret the tiny script, etched with a fairy needle, round the shining rim.

In the end, both dwarf and man knew how to overcome the great Sarkani of the north, but neither was certain Gleb would survive.

Wearing Glockenspiel's ring upon the correct finger at each juncture in battle was crucial. Taking no weapon but the ring was implicit. Boris warned Gleb multiple times over to let no one take it from him by force or by cunning.

Gleb embraced Boris, in spite of his stiffness, and thanked the dwarf for his aid and wisdom. "We will share the rewards together, if honors and treasures there be."

Boris shook his head. "The ring, this short time in my hand, has given me much. I need no other reward. Go and save our forest."

DURING THE WEEKS *spent deciphering the runes, the dragon had moved quite close. It was devouring the land just over the mountains in places where the kingdom of men touched the frontier. Boris chose to sequester himself in his tree and not watch the confrontation. But he could not escape the noise of battle when Gleb and the beast began to brawl.*

The dragon met Gleb with jaws wide open, expecting the usual quick surrender of its prey. Gleb trembled with horror but though his blood ran cold, he did not lose his courage. The befuddled beast lunged again and again at a disappearing, then reappearing, then disappearing, then reappearing foe. At times the man seemed to fly. The roaring fire of dragon's breath for the first time missed its target. Or did it? Nothing—man nor beast, hill nor dale, tree nor flower—had ever escaped the heat of the mighty Sarkani. How was it now made ineffective? The ever-shifting battle was dizzying to a dragon used to nothing but spiritless surrender.

Boris, over the mountains, heard a fearful clap of thunder when Gleb lifted the tip of the Sarkani's great tail aloft. Glockenspiel's ring glittered on his left thumb. As Gwyllion had promised, his hand was imbued with the power to break rocks and shatter walls. With this strength, Gleb, left-handed, impaled the monster through the lower jaw. The dragon's own pointed appendage pierced through its hideous mouth. With a second thrust, Gleb forced the spike up and into the great lizard's brain.

The death struggle of the monster lasted three days and three nights. The writhing tail, yanked free at last from its head, beat the ground with such violence that a ten-mile radius trembled as if from an earthquake. When at length the beast lay quiet, Gleb moved forward and removed its head as a trophy. This he took to the circle of kings.

In her peripheral vision, Hilda noted Wynona's eyes glowing like burning coals. Geraldine looked to Hilda and then Wynona, paying as much mind to her Sarkani companion now as to the story. The heightened tension between the two made the fact that Loretta had gone missing almost an afterthought.

The conqueror was received with great adulation. Gleb's chosen princess needed no convincing, and a magnificent wedding was celebrated within a fortnight with fireworks and parades.

GWYLLION, *meanwhile, was plotting a hellish revenge. She wondered how Gleb expected to live happily-ever-after in the arms of a beautiful princess as a king's son-in-law. How bitterly she rued the day she had ever trusted him. Her fury was tremendous. She had favored a mortal with her love and he had repaid her with treachery and theft. She had required but a drop of blood upon a gemstone. Having long ago forgone her own soul, Gwyllion had no way to understand why Gleb still valued his.*

The dragon lay where Gleb had slain it, and the monstrous body began to rot. The smell emanating from the corpse poisoned the air of multiple kingdoms. Gleb was called upon to solve the problem he had helped create. He decided, once more, to seek the wise advice of Boris.

If Gleb had not been high on young love, he would have been more prudent. He would have walked or ridden with a measure of stealth when traveling back to the forest. Instead, Gleb chose to use the magic ring and fly, and by this Gwyllion found and tracked him. Who, other than the lover that had spurned her, would leap from a turret and glide to a soft landing in the forest? By powers older and darker and swifter than King Glockenspiel's ring, Gwyllion arrived before Gleb at the dwarf's home.

When Gleb knocked, Boris's hand reached out through the window in the trunk of his tree. On its palm Gleb placed Glock-enspiel's ring. But the arm of Boris was no longer attached to Boris himself. The drow-maiden had wasted no time.

"Stop," cried Geraldine.

Hilda looked about. Sometime during the story, Wynona had grown. Or had Geraldine shrunk? Hilda could no longer tell which dragon out-fleshed the other.

"How is it …" said Wynona leaning in, her head above the campfire flames. Tongues of fire now drew back in dread of the greatness of a full-grown Sarkani. "How is it, little girl-human, that the story you weave builds up so nobly the awesomeness of the Sarkani, and then dispatches greatness in less than a page with a flimsy piece of magic jewelry? By what lies do you peoples live, that make your tales build more dread of woman-hood than of dragon?"

Geraldine tried to intervene. "The point of the story, Wynona, is that Gwyllion's womanhood was distracting Gleb's manliness from his noble life mission …"

"Stop!" screamed Wynona. "I am done with your lectures. My people are dishonored. This young human will not tell this tale, or any other, ever again."

"The End," said Hilda flatly. "Thus concludes the tale. The. End."

Both dragons glared.

Hilda stared in return. "Keep. Your. Word."

Both dragons took a step backward.

Wynona looked around. Geraldine unfurled her wings, "I have an appointment to keep. Wynona, come."

Wynona's eyes looked into Hilda's. In that single split second, before shutting fast her lids, the maiden tasted dragon's fire. When Hilda opened her eyes again, she had a splitting headache, but she was alone.

The fire was sputtering out.

The moon was rising high.

From the cabin wafted the smell of raisins steamed in porridge.

Oran was minding the stove.

BABIOLA

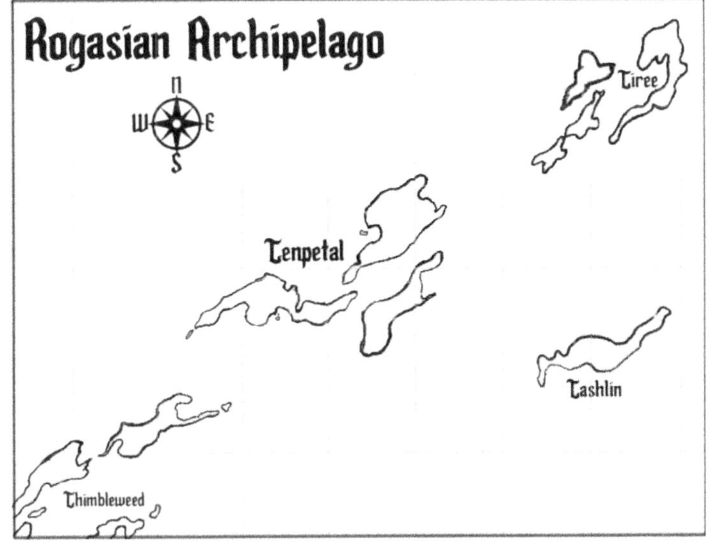

Rogasian Archipelago
N
W E
S
Tiree
Tenpetal
Tashlin
Thimbleweed

[1]

A WISH TO BE MORE WIDELY READ

Three things never satisfied,
Four things never say, "Enough!"
Parched earth, a waiting tomb
Raging fire and barren womb

Queen Valencia sat alone by her fireside, afflicted. The hopeful flames of the morning, reawakened by her stoking, were quickly dying down and joining last night's meager coals. She had been tossing in book after once-favored book. Her impassive face watched tongues of fire lick up page after page. Not even the crackling whine of dogeared passages changed the queen's countenance.

Valencia had just completed five years of satisfactory marriage to King Hubert of Tiree. For five years she had enjoyed leisure: walks in the garden, candy and nuts in the sitting room, and hour upon hour of voracious reading. She had no children to steal her sweets or interrupt her absorption in any given storyline. Now she did not pause to wonder how the destruction of volumes she had once read so enjoyably troubled her so little.

In the beginning of her fifth year of wedlock, Valencia began to hound her husband for different fare. The gardens seemed stunted, the candy stale, and the dozens of books at her disposal seemed to present the same characters and conundrums, again and again. Folks were either motherless, or childless; too good to be true, or too bad to be believable. Plots creative and whimsical, twisted with enchantment, were home to flat characters flopping upon the pages.

Valencia was no longer a princess waiting to be chosen, but a married queen. She was not on the run from wicked parents, but had left her mother and father in a willing and cordial parting. She was not lacking in anything, and had no interest in more gold or jewels. She knew of no dragons lurking in the forests of Tiree.

Perhaps it was the realization that fairy tale characters no longer brought any sense of company. Perhaps she could learn the practical skills of barrel-making or pottery? Gardening? Vineyards? The dark arts? Not, of course, to actually callous her royal hands, but to better supervise those who did. Perhaps the menfolk had books they hoarded for themselves. Valencia became consumed by restless curiosity.

At his queen's requests for broader subject matter, King Hubert dragged his feet. The king did not read[1] and he saw no point in filling his domicile with materials known to be a fire hazard. Candles, oil lamps, parchment, and paper were a well-documented perilous combination. The queen should be making babies. How more books would help in this task, he could not tell.

Hubert, always well-mannered, said not a word of complaint but hid his inward weariness. Night after night, he went to bed with an unfruitful wife who would not cease her fatiguing chatter about new titles and emerging authors. Each evening when they retired, he would roll over in their enormous feather bed and think of how he should have listened to his mother's warnings about taking a wife from a family said to be rife with inbred enchantment.

As a young prince, Hubert had laughed off his mother's fairy magic nonsense. He had found Valencia's ample bosom to be spell enough. Now, more than five years in, he knew he should have scrutinized his wife's eager availability. He should have questioned her willingness to downsize and enter his smaller kingdom. But he heard no warnings because he could think of nothing but bedding her, and the doorway into Valencia's boudoir was matrimony.

Valencia knew somewhere, in places deep down, that books provided her an escape from obvious problems and possible solutions. She more than suspected enchantment was at the core of her marital conflict. She had heard in childhood from old wives wagging their tongues that—though she herself had not been put under a spell—she had been born in spite of one.

A fairy of the highest order, the capricious Sabellia, had cursed Valencia's mother with barrenness. Only prayers and bribes to several kindlier fairies had allowed for a single pregnancy—the one that produced Princess Valencia. To King Hubert's great frustration, the spell meant for Valencia's mother hovered about in its unapplied potency. It seemed to have exerted all its pent-up frustration in full force upon the next generation. King Hubert was the rare husband whose problems really did lay squarely at the feet of his mother-in-law.

As Valencia reached to toss a fifteenth book into the waiting flame, a little old woman no more than a foot tall popped out of the open flue. Flying down against the current of rising smoke, the visitor rode on a loose bundle of rushes and wore in her cap a branch of hawthorn. Her dress was made of the gossamer wings of butterflies; her shoes were carved from two walnut shells. She sailed through the air, thrice round the chamber, and then came in for a landing at the feet of the queen.

"I have heard your murmuring, Majesty," announced the cackling fairy. "You blame me for all your misfortunes. You think that I am the cause of your having no children."

Valencia was dumfounded. She had no memory of saying anything of the kind aloud (though the possibility had wandered through her thoughts for years). Her jaw remained dropped as the intruder continued on with more pronouncements. "I have come to proclaim that you and Hubert will soon have a daughter. But I fear that she will bring you little joy and cost you many tears."

Queen Valencia, knowing no better, opened her heart to the sprite and began to beg. "Ah! Noble Sabellia, have pity! I promise you all the services that lie in my royal power. Only allow the princess you prophesy to be my comfort, and not my affliction."

"Destiny is more powerful than I am," said Sabellia. "All I can do to dampen the prophecy's potency is to give you this sprig of white hawthorn. Wrap it round your daughter's head the instant she is born. It will guard her from many dangers."

The fairy pulled the hawthorn from her cap, placed the branch upon the lap of the silent queen, and vanished like a flash of lightning.

Valencia sat alone, sad and thoughtful. How did this happen? What had she done to deserve such a child? Would it not be better to remain childless? Why this punishment? What strange, unseen magic drew the fairy to her chamber when she had merely been burning books?

Queen Valencia said not a word to her husband about the strange visitation, though he noted that she spoke no more of grand plans for a royal library. Valencia instead shared her troubles with several of her ladies-in-waiting, seeking comfort. None knew what to say or do, except the queen's favorite, Gilda Happenstance. She took the hallowed sprig of hawthorn and, in the presence of all, placed it with great ceremony in a golden lockbox encrusted with diamonds. All the ladies took comfort in the sober formality. Now the item, valued by the queen more than everything else in the world, was in its proper place.

To the king's great pleasure, Valencia became pregnant.

After a long hard labor, a beautiful daughter was born.

Valencia cradled the little princess while Gilda unlatched the gilded box in haste. The queen trembled lest something should happen before the child was under the protection of the hawthorn crown.

The instant the sprig was tied round the infant's head, the longed-for little daughter became a little monkey. Up and away the hairy baby leapt, jumping and skipping round the room. All the ladies uttered dreadful cries. Valencia opened her mouth, but her agony produced only a silent scream.

Gilda alone moved to recapture the creature. After great exertion, abandonment of all decorum, and the overturning of much furniture, the tiny animal was wrestled and pinned. But when the panting handmaid unfastened and removed the fatal hawthorn from the head of the newborn princess, there was not the least change.

She remained a furry little monkey.

She would not nestle in her mother's arms but leapt away

to feast upon the fresh fruit and nuts brought in for the refreshment of the queen.

Queen Valencia at last found her voice. "Barbarous, treacherous, Sabellia! What have I done?" She buried her face in her pillows and wept. "What will become of me? What a disgrace when all my subjects find out that I have given birth to a beast! What will the king think?"

When Her Majesty at last fell silent, Gilda Happenstance addressed her in an almost commanding tone, "Madam, your husband the king must be told that the princess is dead. Give orders that this brutish animal be done away with, and I will see it accomplished."

Queen Valencia said nothing in reply. She sat and shook and held her silence for over an hour. Her ladies watched, eyes peeled for any sign of instruction. Meanwhile, the monkey hopped about eating everything, excreting everywhere, and vocalizing gibberish to accompany her every impulsivity. Just as the ladies began to wonder if their sovereign queen would ever speak again, word came that King Hubert was making his way towards the room, intending to see his wife and newborn. A grave dilemma filled the chamber.

Valencia at last let out a whisper, "Gilda ... do as you think best with the little monkey." She then fell into a dead faint and did not reawaken for many days.

[2]

LITTLE MONKEY NEARLY DEAD

Tenpetal boasts a beautiful city,
All the girls therein are pretty
Little boys go out to dip their oars
Close in to the shallow shores
But men sail off in ships I'm told,
Trading peacocks and monkeys
For silver and gold

Gilda Happenstance, though a woman of action, possessed a sense of irony. She gripped the baby monkey—stomach stuffed and lethargic—by the nape of its neck and deposited the furry creature into the very box that had hours earlier held the hawthorn crown. She ordered a lesser maid to build up the fire and called for a footman to come in haste. Into the fire she tossed the wreath; into the arms of the waiting footman she placed the monkey box.

Minutes before Hubert the King entered, Felix the footman exited. His orders were to walk out upon the great western Pier of King Pibrac and toss the bejeweled chest into the depths. Felix was pleased that Mistress Happenstance, in her hastiness, had not specified *how* he was to travel. Empowered by borrowed authority he barked out his own orders to a loitering stablehand, "Prepare me a pony with a newly shined saddle! Pack saddlebags with cheese and grapes. I go out on important business!"

As Hubert came into the queen's chamber, it was slowly filling with smoke. Gilda turned and saw the hawthorn had not gone up in flames but held its shape and smoldered defiantly. A draft was pushing the fumes back down the flue, causing all within the room to choke. When the king began to cough as well, Gilda motioned for His Majesty to follow her back out into the hallway. He went with her in haste and there received the tragic news about the infant's death and his wife's weakness.

While Gilda spoke without, her underlings within moved to open windows and smother what remained of the misbehaving fire. Within the hearth the ladies saw a single burning coal surrounded by a perfect ring of deep purple ash. When they looked a second time, the purple ash had vanished.

HALFWAY TO THE SEASHORE, footman Felix abandoned his pony. The young man was not used to riding and now, far from home, the blisters forming on his buttocks were no longer soothed by the admiration of his fellow servants. The chestnut bay turned and trotted back to the stables. Felix draped the saddlebag over his right arm, wedged the gilded box under his left, and proceeded on foot.

When at last he came in sight of the sea, Felix knelt to rest, finding (with some difficulty) a position that would take pressure off both his chafed posterior and tired feet. Thankful for the refreshing grapes and cheese, he arose once more, clutching the box in both hands, and continued his obedient journey. The footman took his first steps upon the wide beach just as the sun began to sink.

Felix had heard that the kingdom of Tiree was one of many islands in the Rogasian Archipelago, stretching for hundreds of miles east and west. But he had never before stood on the shore and pondered the great expanse of ocean. He was a young man under authority, always running hither and thither at someone else's beck and call, a small player on a small island of little import. He stood awestruck.

The box he held firmly glimmered in the fading sunlight. The wide sea shimmered with every rising wave. Glancing back and forth, Felix felt the strange tragedy of one beauty devouring another. Sparkle would meet sparkle and then the box would sink beneath the waves. Why throw such a treasure away when what mattered lay inside? Who would know? Who would care if he dumped the contents and kept the container?

The footman seated himself on the seashore, took out his penknife, and pried open the locked lid. Felix possessed no inborn tenderness towards animals, but when inside he found a tiny monkey sound asleep, he felt strangely moved. Perhaps he could kill the creature quickly before casting it into the ocean. A quick break of the neck might be a tender mercy.

Felix cradled the sleeping animal and approached the great Pibrac Pier, built by the famed conquerer-builder of old. The boards creaked as he stepped out over the waves. A dozen steps took him halfway. The sun sank, the waves glimmered. The monkey turned and threaded a tiny finger through the footman's belt loop.

As he walked, Felix noted a small boat with a single raised sail approaching from the north. A green banner atop the mast was edged in purple. Upon it billowed the flapping shape of a ten-petaled blossom white as sea foam with a golden center. The sound of music came from the deck. Felix became enamored by the sad beauty in the tune. By the time he reached the end of the pier, he had forgotten his errand. He stood dumbly listening and watching the sailboat's smooth approach, running softly before a tailwind.

On the cushions of the stern sat a man of royal personage, holding a lute. Noting that he was watched, the regal young man saluted. Felix clutched the monkey and bowed. He half-recalled the floral emblem as that of the neighboring kingdom.

The closer the little boat came to the pier, the more the footman sensed he was a secret part of a grander story. He became certain the pilot of the boat was keeping a preplanned rendezvous. To pry open the bejeweled chest was a test of his intuition, and to lay the monkey into the waiting arms of the arriving prince had surely been his clandestine mission all along.

For his part, the Crown Prince of Tenpetal, accustomed to receiving gifts from unnamed subjects, played his part fittingly in the Felix's fantasy. He took the baby monkey without a word and turned his ship back towards home. As soon as the boat pointed seaward, the monkey awoke, reached up, and gently played with the prince's ample nose.

Footman Felix gained a coin for his troubles and the last thing he heard as the boat sailed out of sight and earshot was, "You are the prettiest creature I have ever beheld. I shall call you Babiola and you shall live with me in the palace. Wait until my sisters see you! They shall be filled with envy and delight."

Felix felt a tear of joy trickle down his cheek as he turned back towards the beach. There he retrieved the golden box and knew he had done his quiet part in something grand.

[3]

SEVENTH-BORN WITH STATELY NOSE

Head, shoulders, knees, nose
Watch closely how the young prince grows
Be he tall or be he stout
Admire only the royal snout

Prince Septimius had thick hair, bright eyes, and perfect lips. He would have been handsome if not for his nose. There was, without doubt, material enough in his oversized snout to make three reasonable sets of nostrils.

Queen Maureen had desperately wanted her seventh pregnancy to produce a son, and her favorite fairy, Marcionna, owed her a favor. Marcionna—who abhorred small noses on the faces of men—overdid a portion of her charm when she wove an incantation over the belly of the queen.

Maureen's pregnancy was without incident. After his birth, the newborn boy was easily contented. But the royal labor required to give entrance to the seventh royal offspring was full of fits and starts. The infant's nose made the exiting of his cranium complicated.

During her first nursing[1] of her son, Queen Maureen called Fairy Marcionna into account for the oversized proboscis.

"I asked for a son, not a woodpecker," Maureen growled.

"It is for his character development, Your Majesty," answered Marcionna as if reading a script.

"Who put you in charge of formation of character?" said the queen. "As if his father and I are not capable!"

"He is an only son, my lady. I have lived several centuries, and believe me, only sons are in great peril—especially with so many sisters coming before. It is the way of things."

"But why such a nose! It is overdone!" protested Maureen. "Is it permanent?"

"All will be made right, my queen, when he humbly acknowledges the flaw."

Queen Maureen pondered these words for a moment and humphed, "A man never acknowledges his defects until they become obstacles to his wishes."

"With six sisters to dote on him and grant his every whim, your prince needs a defect that could prove an obstacle. It is an absolute necessity," said Marcionna.

Queen Maureen moved her swollen breast round her baby's spacious nose so the infant could suckle properly. As she watched him gulp she began to cry.

Marcionna exited and maids-in-waiting took her place. Each offered a word of consolation.

"It's not so large, Your Majesty."

"It's a Roman nose, your grace."

"History has many heroes with large noses, my queen."

Maureen, who already loved her son to excess, was charmed by these words. The more she stared at Septimius, the less obtrusive his nose became.

The little prince was brought up very carefully. As soon as he could speak, all kinds of shocking stories were told to him of people who had short noses. Servants with short noses were fired and replaced with those with long ones. Courtiers began to pull their children's noses several times a day hoping to lengthen them.

When Septimius became old enough for school, his history lessons were adjusted. Whenever any great prince or handsome princess was mentioned, he or she was always spoken of as having a large nose. The prince grew so accustomed to regarding length of nose as a prized ornament, he could not imagine taking advice from a pug-faced savant, nor lessons in artistry from a button-nosed virtuoso. And a future bride who could not match him in size, nostril for nostril, was unthinkable.

ALL OF THE ROYAL CHILDREN, by explicit directive of King Egbert, were named according to birth order in Latin: Prima, Secunda, Tertia, Quarta, Quinta, Sexta; and, at last, the afore-mentioned only son, Septimius.

The king loved nothing better than to call out his children's Latin names and line them up in a little royal regiment. Queen Maureen, having gained her husband's permission to insert middle names in alphabetical order, loved the fact that her creative addition caused the six princesses of the Tenpetal Islands to have monikers that formed a poem—

> *Prima Adela*
> *Secunda Brigitta*
> *Tertia Carlita*
> *Quarta Dephella,*
> *Quinta Elita*
> *Sexta Finita*

Septimius was given the middle name Gilbert, a fact that he tried to ignore.

The awkwardness of the Latin name given to his sixth daughter—Sexta Finita—had not deterred King Egbert's drive for systemization in the least, but everyone in the palace followed the queen's example and called her Finita.[2]

Septimius, the year before entering adolescence, decided to become a sailor. His mother begged him to take up hunting on the eastern island, or fishing from the western shore, but her only son had found a never-before-known freedom on the deck of a beautiful little boat. It was his only place of respite from over-mothering by one, and over-sistering by six.

To each of the female worries Septimius had a ready answer.

"The pirates!" wept his mother.

"I have a cutlass," was his curt reply.

"Undertows and unknown currents!" cried Prima, wringing both hands.

"I can swim as well as any man," Septimius would retort.

"There are sea monsters that would love nothing better than to dine upon a prince," called out the creative imaginings of Secunda.

"Only in your dreams," laughed her little brother.

"Stinging jellyfish!" cried Tertia.

"Sharks!" wailed Quarta.

"Whales!" lamented Quinta.

"My singing is a terror, and they shall all scurry away," Septimius chortled.

"Take me with you," whispered Sexta.

"No, Finita, no, a man needs his time alone," the prince would answer flatly and listen no more.

All the worries of sisters and mother were, in truth, well-founded. Pirates captured, sea monsters swallowed, jellyfish stung, undercurrents pulled under, sharks dismembered, and whales capsized vessels great and small. In fact, neither mother nor sisters had imagined half the dangers lurking among the multitude of islands in the unexplored reaches of the Rogasian Archipelago. Numerous beyond counting were the hazards that threatened the little boat that bore their brother every time he pushed merrily from shore.

But Septimius's need to find his way through reef and storm was more pressing than the well-founded anxieties of a thousand women. In fact his little boat, the *Morning Star*, saved Tenpetal's Crown Prince from the subtle and sickly undertow lapping at the feet of all well-to-do young men. If Septimius had made it his chief aim to please the women who loved him so, he would have spent his young years occupied by trifles. His mind would have been trained in pomp and circumstance, food and finery, drink and dinnerware, organic ingredients and hors d'oeuvres. His opinions would have been wrapped around professing passions where he felt none, repeating to peers news he heard elsewhere, memorizing witticisms to keep up with the times, and showing off his jewels and other finery put in reach by his princely allowance.

Septimius's father was often absent. The king did little to instruct him. But Egbert put a hard boundary between his son and womanly interference. *Morning Star* and prince Septimius were not to be parted. As long as he filed a charted course with the steward, his son's desire to sail was not to be thwarted.

[4]

WALK UPRIGHT IN REGAL CLOTHES

Little one can hide no longer
Pulled from shadows once her haunt
The more she knows, the more she knows
She cannot have the thing she wants

When the sisters of Prince Septimius first saw the little monkey in his arms, they begged to have her as a playmate. And while he did not give up all rights of custody, he allowed them oversight of Babiola any time he went out to sail.

Never was there a more agreeable well-mannered little monkey than Babiola. Her face was jet black, a white frill encompassed her neck, and tufts of red hair crowned her ears. Her hands were skillful and her eyes shone bright with vivacious intelligence and untapped talent. The princesses took great delight in dressing her like themselves and ordered new clothes made for her every week. To please their governess, and gain access for the monkey into their school room, they taught her to walk upright upon her hind feet.

Babiola enjoyed all six princesses, but it was Prince Septimius who won her heart. Every evening she would race back to his quarters to sleep. When he laughed, she chattered with happiness. When he cried, on occasion, he swore he saw tears in her eyes also.

The flat-faced monkey loved him and overlooked his ungainly nose, giving it no second thought.

TENPETAL WAS a group of three isles under a single ruler, a rare show of cohesion in the politically fractured archipelago. While Septimius wove in and out of the island chain in his little sloop, Prima, Secunda, Tertia, Quarta, Quinta, and Finita never—even once—ventured out of sight of their palace home.

Upon the central island, a sprawling chateau had been built high up on a cliffside, out of reach of the tempestuous sea and unpredictable buccaneers. King Egbert dreaded that one of his six daughters might be taken by the archipelago pirates known to prowl the currents between the islands and shanghai the unwary. Hubert forbade his girls from ever exiting the castle grounds without proper military escort—an escort he never found funds to provide.

The king did his best to make up for his daughters' lack of freedom by giving over to them the largest wing of the castle. He also planted an extraordinary garden, covering the entirety of forty-nine acres, for their exploration and entertainment. Free rein of the annex and full liberty within the acreage gave five out of the six princesses a sense of a rich, fulfilled life. The wooded paradise only increased the longing in the heart of Finita to go to sea with her little brother.

The palace garden was a wonder, ideally situated for sun and fresh air. Tall pines and firs were planted and pruned to give a sense of wildness even within the confining walls.

Peasant children were let in twice a week, a few at a time, to play with the royals. These guests ran about chattering, doing their best to cater to royal whims in hopes of being invited again.

"What a pretty princess you are!"

"Oh how lucky you are to be a daughter of the king!"

These flatteries rolled off the backs of five out of the six princesses. They irritated Finita like sand in a sandwich. She would take Babiola in her arms and saunter off into the woods where together they would follow the brook that ran in, and out, and in again under the walls. Finita would imagine fairies floating by on large leaves with their bodyguards fighting off tiny pirates trying to capture them. Babiola would climb the nearby trees and enjoy her acrobatic prowess.

Just before sundown, the village children would file out and the princesses would line up—in birth order, as was tradition. After marching in, they would sup together, and the little monkey would return to the wing occupied by Prince Septimius.

During Babiola's fourth year at Tenpetal Hall, King Hubert had a hawthorn tree planted in the middle of the garden acreage where the soil drained well and the sun always shone. Babiola eyed it curiously. By late spring the hawthorn had taken root, shooting upward in a breathtaking spurt and beginning to lord itself over the older trees. Babiola never climbed into its branches, but every evening, when the children were called to go in, she would approach the young hawthorn, wrap the newest shoot round her delicate paw, and pull ever so slightly. Upon release, the newly forming branch would reverberate against the trunk. Babiola would not break away her gaze until all motion ceased.

No one seemed to notice this peculiar obsessive predictability but Finita.

The following fall, on a day when no guests were let in, Babiola surprised Finita by springing from her shoulder during a stroll, dashing to the highest branch of the hawthorn and staring out over the distant waves. Finita's whole being resonated with a strange sympathetic longing as she strained her eyes and ears to take in the new behavior. A downward draft brought to the ears of the princess an incongruent sound. She thought she heard a stammering child trying to form first words.

Finita called to Babiola, and the before now ever-courageous monkey returned to her at once, trembling and clutching about her keeper's neck. Finita was sure, when she told the story later, that it was in that moment she heard Babiola speak her first word: "home."

To Finita's amazement, what came next was a clear sweet voice. The little monkey quoted an oft-heard poem with distinct elocution.

> *Tenpetal boasts a beautiful city,*
> *All the girls therein are pretty*

Finita overlooked her long-standing disdain for that particular couplet. She forgot her deep-rooted fondness for secrecy, and galloped back to where her sisters were gathered together. Jostling the stunned little monkey with every footfall she cried out, "Babiola is speaking! Babiola is speaking!"

If Finita had known what would happen afterward, she would have tried with all her might to keep the miracle concealed.

From that day on, all was changed.

Babiola was no longer the children's pet. Now both the king and the queen wanted the monkey for their own amusement. She was all at once the gem of Tenpetal, the talk of the kingdom, a monkey of great fame, and her renown began to spread across the whole wide archipelago.

To console her, Finita was given three dogs, two cats, eight birds, four squirrels, and even a little horse which danced the cha cha. But she would have preferred Babiola—even before she could speak—to the lot of them, fifty times over.

For Babiola, the change was more than repugnant.

All at once, she was required to answer like a sage to a hundred ingenious questions. Whenever a foreign ambassador arrived, she was dressed in a velvet gown covered in brocade with a frill round her neck, and shown off like a vaudeville act. She was no longer allowed to forage and eat when and what she wished, but given food prescribed with careful calculation by the court physician.

Queen Maureen appointed Babiola tutors and trainers to attune her simian tongue to fluency in several languages. Her nimble fingers were taught to play a dozen pieces on the harpsichord. Artists came from foreign lands to draw her portrait. Her name and likeness spread from island to island.

Once the most beloved palace pet, Babiola became a highly managed showpiece. Her soul shrank under the overbearing expectations and ever-tightening rules of etiquette. Wallowing in confused futility, the little monkey—born a princess—contrived ways to resist.

Prince Septimius, graceful, ingenious, and incredibly handsome (except for his nose), visited Babiola often at court. The conversations between them were witty and lively, sometimes taking a serious philosophical or spiritual turn. Babiola's heart was not monkeyish like the rest of her little person, and she became very attached to the prince—too attached.

While Babiola became fonder and fonder of Septimius, Septimius became fonder and fonder of hunting, dancing, weaponry, and navigation. He thought of the little monkey only when he was conversing directly with her. When she would reproach him for his neglect, he would bring her a rosy apple or a handful of roasted chestnuts, believing these actions made up for his forgetfulness. When Septimius felt idle or bored, he would sneak Babiola from his mother's sitting room and hide her in his own quarters. His attendants would often laugh at the monkey's grave face when she was asked to provide amusement for the Crown Prince and his friends.

Sometimes, all the depth that passed between herself and the prince in private conversation was so wonderful that Babiola did not know what to do. The nights became impossible. She would refuse her silk-lined basket and spend the night on the top of a wide window cornice, or tucked in a chimney corner. Her governess often heard her sigh, sometimes complain, and, on occasion, even weep. Her melancholy only increased as her mind expanded.

Every time Babiola saw her monkey-self in a looking-glass, she would become vexed and strive to break it. The courtiers took this as opportunity to reduce her to a proverb, "A monkey will always be a monkey. Babiola, with all her talents, cannot rid herself of the malicious temper of her species."

[5]

CRASHING CHANGE AND PIRATE LUST

I'm dying, monkey dear, for you!
Bored of ships and pirate booty
Come see the treats my ships abound in
To make you welcome is my duty
Figs and fruits to please you well,
Come be our honored monkey belle.

The estrogen-filled wing of Tenpetal Hall was lit up with excitement. Both Prima and Secunda were newly engaged to dashing princes on far-off isles. Queen Maureen swooned in traumatized joy while Finita envied both sisters' coming freedom. The constant talk of plans and preparations stole all the youngest princess's pleasure usually found in sunshine and trees, birds and brook. Even in the rose-colored clouds that sailed over at dawn and at sunset gave her none of the usual joy.

That autumn, during the feast of St. Hilda, Tertia announced her intention to enter a monastery. Queen Maureen raised one brow, King Egbert furrowed two. A shiver went through Quarta and Quinta as they took in the crash of change. The table would soon have three empty places. Finita pondered how she might stow away in anyone's baggage to escape the repetitive repression of home.

Winter came, and the snow lay white and sparkling all round. Babiola slipped from the throne room and came out to play, springing happily in front of Finita's footfalls like old times. But the princess felt little more than annoyance in the breaking up of the perfect surface of a newly fallen snow. She was lost in thought, mulling over how next year she would be several inches taller and, being so nearly grown, her life might finally begin.

Forcing a smile, the princess turned to Babiola and asked her friend to climb to the highest branch of a nearby tree. "Please report to me all you see, wide and far."

Babiola ascended and peered out into the wide horizon. In the clear cloudless air, hazy shapes of sailing ships under splendid sails moved upon the depths. "Ah! They are grand!" she called out, then caught herself, remembering Finita's distress-filled longing.

Babiola climbed down and sat upon Finita's shoulder.

"What sort of ships did you see?" questioned Finita. "How big? How fast? How far is it to where the sky touches the sea? Or, does horizon go on without end?"

Babiola sighed and cleared her throat. "Well ... what I saw looks like forever, but ... not everything is as it seems. Rejoice in the loving protection that guards you, Finita. Rejoice in the unbroken heart beating within."

Babiola hopped to the ground, took Finita by the hand, and led the young princess back towards the palace. A monkey tear rolled down a monkey cheek with only the wind to kiss it.

To be neither animal nor human was becoming unbearable.

THE FAME OF BABIOLA—SAVANT of the kingdom of Tenpetal —reached the wild edges of the sea's horizon. Dread pirate Nestorio pulled her portrait from the arms of a traveling artist and was captivated in a single glance by her face, framed by the white frilled collar. It had been Captain Nestorio's habit to toss artifacts overboard and keep prisoners to sell but, with his coffers full and his favorite woman newly buried, he reversed his usual course of action. He learned all he could from the sniveling artist about the fascinating countenance, then tossed the prisoner overboard and held onto the portrait. The de facto emperor of the Rogasian Archipelago, casting about for some-thing new to occupy his passions, was seized by a violent craving to have the noble little monkey join the crew of the blackmarket armada.

Nestorio could not travel to fetch his desired prize himself. He had serious repairs to both his ships and his reputation to attend to. Three of his largest galleons had sprung leaks, and five of his seamen had been caught helping themselves to protection money. Occupied by pitch and tar and keelhauling, he sent his chief emissary, Pelagio, in his stead. Pelagio, both shrewd and loyal, would achieve his ends whatever barriers were thrown down to obstruct. The henchman, a lumbering hulk, had a nimble mind.

PELAGIO ARRIVED by first-class carriage with a troop of finely dressed pideser monkeys, recently fished from the coastal waters of Tiree.[1] The unlikely ambassador planned to woo and court favor, not threaten and blackmail—at least not at first. The monkey troop, he would say, was destined to attend and serve Babiola like the royalty she was. Would she not honor the pirate's court on the island of Thimbleweed with her presence?

King Egbert and Queen Maureen had no warning of the approach of the mysterious envoy until the ship landed at the harbor only a few miles from their palace door. From a high balcony the king and queen spied a colossal man with an apelike gait, surrounded by a half-dozen chittering monkeys. Both wanted to laugh, but had a sense that something somber was about to pierce their domestic tranquility.

King Egbert, fully confident in his wife's abilities as hostess, whispered in her ear a single phrase about security at the docks and the whereabouts of Septimius. His Majesty slipped out a back entrance, leaving the queen to greet the visiting emissary alone.

Queen Maureen stood tall. Pelagio stopped, looked up, and bellowed. His voice carried the distance with little effort, "Your Majesty! I beg audience regarding business of the utmost importance."

"Noble stranger," called back the queen. "You had better first take some refreshment. We shall meet before nightfall in the throne room."

Pelagio was received cordially by palace servants, and brought to an apartment to await audience with the queen. He had no sooner entered the waiting room when his consort of monkeys scattered to ferret out sweetmeats. Pelagio paid no mind. While the gluttons dumped pots and jars, shattered glasses of apricot preserves, and overturned several trays of poppyseed pastries, Pelagio flopped upon the wide yellow settee and lost no time downing an entire box of chocolates himself.

When the ambassador at last made his entrance into the throne room, he strode with such confidence that the courtiers forgot he was not dressed in any way in the fashion of the day.

Pelagio's wardrobe was Nestorio's cast-offs and Nestorio was a much smaller man. Lumbering Pelagio cut an impressive figure in his boss's blue pointed hat adorned with a green feather. Over a red vest, which was covered in golden spangles, he wore a purple shoulder belt. His brown pants were drawn up round his knees, showing thick stockings held in place by large ribbons of green, not quite the same shade as the feather.

Pelagio removed his cap and bowed low to the queen, then again, even lower, to Babiola. Maureen understood his intentions in a flash and set course for a long, drawn out, stately stalling. She was well versed in the use of charm for the sake of buying time. Babiola, despite her stoic exterior, trembled with a foreboding, not unlike the fateful day she was endowed with speech.

Pelagio told the queen before all the court of how Babiola's fame had reached his master's ears. He trumpeted how the dread pirate Nestorio had sent his servant to make the esteemed monkey's acquaintance. He, Pelagio, had come charged to extend an official invitation for Mistress Babiola to visit his master. And, if the wondrous monkey liked the change of scene, she could stay as an honored guest, however, with whomever, and in whatever manner she liked.

Everyone present knew there would be no coming back, but none showed a hint of feeling. Pelagio's smooth speech promised several enticing gifts to the kingdom of Tenpetal in general and to Queen Maureen in particular. He ended his appeal with a song for the famed Babiola purported to have been written by Nestorio himself. (Yes, that is it in the chapter opening.)

Queen Maureen listened to the emissary's flattering words, but gave no answer that could be construed as agreement. Her Majesty kept expressing how dearly she loved the monkey's company, how sweet Babiola was, what comfort she brought, how she could not imagine life without her.

By the end of the appointment, the queen told Pelagio she must think it over, and could decide on nothing without consulting with her very busy husband.

Pelagio smiled.

"I must return to Captain Nestorio in three days time, Your Majesty," answered the henchman, bowing. "And I, as do so many, fear disappointing my master."

[6]

SOME TO LOVE BUT NOT TO TRUST

Some walls keep out,
Some hold all in
Some bold-face lie,
Some hedge and spin
Some, on finger wrapped around
Will open up, and then shut down

"My little monkey," said Queen Maureen to Babiola, as soon as the two of them were alone, "I must confess that I shall be very sorry to part with you."

Babiola, standing like a soldier at attention, waited for a wave of shock to tremor through her, only to realize that she was not at all astounded.

The queen continued, "There is grave danger in denying the great pirate Nestorio what he desires. I will speak to King Egbert but I already know his answer. Still, asking will allow you a small window of time to adjust."

"How are you so certain of the king's mind?" queried Babiola in a tone flat and cold.

"My husband," said Maureen, "has not yet recovered from his *last* altercation with the pirates."

The queen sighed and continued in a nostalgic tone, "In the years before our first child was born, Egbert left my side but once. He went out to engage in a fierce naval battle, only to have the brigands sink so many of our valiant ships that he was obliged to conclude a shameful peace. How lucky our little kingdom was to have my Egbert return to us!"

"What I am hearing you say, madam," said Babiola, "is that the matter is already decided. You have resolved to sacrifice me to this vile monster in order to avoid conflict. I entreat Your Majesty, however, to grant me at least a delay of a few days, so I might resolve myself to the fact I can be traded away like any other royal pet."

"I've already said I would buy you time," huffed the queen. "Don't be selfish. Think of the girls. Think of Septimius! Consider the honors that await you, and the magnificent pirate treasure. The monkeys who now accompany Pelagio are but a foretaste of your entourage."

The queen now broke with all etiquette and stooped to look Babiola straight in the eye. "Keep in mind, my dear little monkey, that here in the kingdom of Tenpetal you have never been assigned more than a single servant at a time, and none of those who served you were under your authority. You will have your first real taste of power and, believe me, it is intoxicating."

"I do not know enough of Ambassador Pelagio to trust his words," replied Babiola quietly, "but I know that even if his fulfillment were twice what he has promised, it moves me very little."

With these words, Babiola gave a little graceful curtsey and left the room.

Down the hall the little monkey wandered in search of Prince Septimius, hoping to pour out her sorrows. The prince saw her coming down the long hallway towards his suite. "Well, Babiola," he called out, "I hear we shall be bidding you farewell, that a world of opportunity has opened itself up before your agile feet!"

"I do not know, sir," said Babiola, hunched and sorrowful.

"Come into my quarters, little monkey, and cheer up."

Babiola entered. The prince flopped into his favorite chair while his diminutive friend, like a serious old man, began to pace. At last Babiola stopped, stood up straight, and faced Septimius.

"I find myself in so deplorable a condition that it is no longer in my power to withhold my heart's true feelings from you. I must confess that you are the only future I have ever desired. As asinine as it may seem, I have long loved you and dreamt of marriage."

"Me? Your husband!" said the prince, bursting into a loud laugh. "Husband indeed! My little monkey, though I am charmed at what you say, excuse me for my laughter at your confession. In truth, we are not suited to each other in height, looks, or manners."

Septimius noticed neither Babiola's blinking away of tears, nor the stoic closing down of all expression of emotion.

"Hearing your response, I all at once agree," replied Babiola, "for I can no longer deny that most especially our hearts are unsuited. I now feel the foolishness of having affection for a prince who is so unworthy of it. You are an ingrate. I have long perceived it but, until now, ignored all evidence."

"But, Babiola," laughed Septimius, "think now, if we married, of all the anxiety I would feel to see you at the top of a sycamore tree, hanging from a branch by your tail. Think of how your species ages twice as fast mine. Take my advice. Let us laugh at this affair for the sake of your honor and my own. Go choose a monkey among the pirates. I hear several are circus-trained and, though speechless, are quite talented. Next year, as a token of the good friendship between us, send me your first baby."

"It is fortunate for you, sir," said Babiola, "that I am not quite a monkey in my mind. Any creature controlled by animal instincts would have already scratched out your eyes, torn off your ears, and bitten a third nostril in your ridiculous nose. I leave your company, hoping you will reflect one day on your unworthy conduct."

Septimius could think of nothing to say and Babiola could say no more, for her governess had come to fetch her. Ambassador Pelagio had delivered magnificent presents to her apartment and she was bid to come and see.

THE GIFTS from Nestorio included a set of handkerchiefs made of silk fine as spider web. Each was embroidered with little fireflies in threads that shimmered. Set beside these, out in a row, was a pincushion shaped like a cherry, bordered in fine lace, a summer bonnet with long orange ribbons, and a raspberry-colored woolen winter beret. On the end table was a green and yellow basket woven from lily leaves, containing mother-of-pearl earrings with a matching necklace as brilliant as starlight. Lastly, laid across the settee, were a dozen boxes of exotic candies. Babiola rifled through them but she had no appetite. She noted a little glass container, shimmering halfway between ruby red and sky blue. What it contained, Babiola could not find out, for the lid was sealed tight.

Pelagio, who stood by watching, informed the monkey—as she lifted and inspected each gift—that his master, the Dread

Pirate Nestorio, was more moved by her charms than he had ever been by those of any other. He was building a palace for her on the island of Thimbleweed, modeled after a treehouse he had once seen in his travels east. Nestorio was also constructing a magnificent stage from which to feature Babiola's harpsichord and oratory skills. "A world tour is being planned and you, dear monkey, will be famous within and without all the wide currents of the Rogasian Archipelago. As Nestorio rules all seas, you shall rule all hearts. Envision and dream with us, dear Babiola. Does not a brilliant primate like yourself deserve more than to be the court mascot on this back-water island?"

Babiola turned her face to look out the window, away from the disagreeable guest. Pelagio paused and shifted his weight. Babiola took a deep breath and answered, "I am honored by your master's esteem, ambassador sir. But I have been treated well here and have not yet made up my mind whether I will stay or go."

Pelagio bowed and scooted backward out the door. As he exited, Babiola turned and noticed that Princess Finita had been listening in, tucked just beyond the door facing. Her eyes glowed with wild excitement and her mouth was agape in inquisitive discovery.

Pelagio now gone, Finita rushed in and took Babiola into her arms, "You are leaving me as well, little monkey?!" she cried.

Babiola shrugged and jumped back down to the floor. Answering nothing, she took Finita by the hand and took her back towards the window. With shuffling steps, Finita whispered a little rhyme that pulsed with a rhythm made for young girls jumping rope—

Prima, Secunda have left and wed

Straw and hay fill Quinta's head
Tertia leaves us next full moon
Babiola, Babiola not so soon …

"You forgot to include Quarta in your jingle," observed Babiola.

"Let's not talk of Quarta. Quarta thinks I'm a baby."

"Have you come to watch me pack?"

"Everyone is going! My sisters are not that much bigger than I! And *you* are smaller," retorted Finita, voice rising. "Little brother is given freedom and I, who used to carry him on my hip, am a prisoner in this dreary palace!"

The monkey nodded once but said not a word.

"Oh Babiola!" Finita continued, "I heard what the ambassador offered you. Imagine being on the stage! You will attain great splendor and magnificence, the adoration of doting fans, and have all the most beautiful delicious things—apples and sweetmeats to your heart's content! They shall dress you in a thousand beautiful costumes."

"And then?" said Babiola, all four limbs trembling. "And then? What happens then?"

"Oh, I can't imagine anything more than that," said Finita. "But what I *can* imagine is simply matchless!"

"How about *you* go then?" mumbled the monkey.

"Don't tease me. If only … " Finita stuttered with excitement, "to … to … to go … to go sailing over the sea! I am sick with longing. If only … "

Babiola looked up at her friend. "Rejoice in your home, Princess. Rejoice in your well-fed youth. Rejoice in the open air and sunshine."

Finita did not hear.

She was trying on the opalescent earrings.

MOONLIGHT PIER AND PALACE GATES

On Morning Star, come sail away with me
Under the moon, perhaps we'll tack towards old Tiree
Though tiller swings aside and ensign tangles in the mast
Shall we turn the prow away and reach her far and fast?
I wonder if returning would do my foundling any harm
Is it wise to take her back to where they laid her in my arms?

Queen Maureen received a note from her husband, delivered by the harbormaster himself. Marauding ships patrolled the mouth of the bay. The fate of a single monkey required no more debate. Maureen would send Babiola where she intended Babiola should go. All remaining threads of indecision unraveled, preparations for the palace pet's departure began.

Upon seeing her belongings rearranged and sorted, despair took entire possession of Babiola. Prince Septimius's contempt gnawed at her heart, Queen Maureen's indifference preyed upon at her mind, and her life at court was now sprawled out and rummaged through by maids and butlers. A veil, thick and heavy, ensconced the little monkey's tender heart and her eyes grew dull.

All that was left to her was a grim determination to escape.

Escape for Babiola was not a difficult thing. Ever since she had begun to speak, she was neither tied up nor caged in. She was the only palace pet to come and go as she pleased, and she entered and exited her room as often by the window as by the door.

That evening as the sun set, Pirate Pelagio thought he saw the shadow of a small figure traveling away from the chateau, high and fast across the cliffside. Near midnight he awoke, certain the motion he had seen was that of his newly-acquired monkey. Dressed only in his skivvies, the pirate ambassador rushed towards Babiola's quarters, pushing past every night maid and watchman in his way.

When he arrived out of breath, Pelagio was not surprised to find Babiola gone. But he *was* surprised to find Princess Finita decked out in the monkey's newly acquired jewelry, stuffing her belly with the monkey's gifted chocolates. His first impulse was to press the maiden for answers, but he set aside the urge to interrogate and took a new tack into winds of opportunity. A talking monkey might have slipped through his fingers but a royal princess had fallen into his hands. He would not leave Tenpetal without a prize worth crowing about.

Unworthy conduct?! ... Ridiculous nose?! thought Septimius, remembering again the parting words of Babiola. The Crown Prince was not one for reflecting, but a monkey confessing her love was a difficult conversation to set aside. "I have a wonderful nose," he assured himself. "And, unlike my sisters, I am not duped by palace flatterers who praise shamelessly while concealing royal defects. I know my flaws, and my nose is not among them."

Still, Septimius could not rest. Something was abuzz in the palace—someone or something had gone missing. At midnight he arose, dressed, and went out walking. A profound change was afoot and he had learned long ago to distance himself from family intrigue. After pacing the garden paths, he left the confinement of the walls and strolled towards the docks to see *Morning Star*. He found her loosely tied and begging for a moonlight sail.

IT WAS easy to take Finita by the hand and lead her quietly where Pelagio intended her to go. Two simple phrases were enamoring magic, "Babiola has refused my offer: Would you like to come in her stead?"

Finita went placidly out into the night and boarded the pirate's first-class carriage. Consumed with thoughts of her coming happiness, the young princess made no room for the sadness of departure. No synapses had been formed in her short life so far that were capable of calculating the cost of forsaking all. She knew no emotion that applied to a departure from one's birthplace, parents, and siblings with no thought of ever seeing them again. In Finita's brain, home was mundane wallpaper peeling in the corners of her royal bedroom, and the pattern in the fading carpet running through the entrance hall. She made no sound but for a barely audible groan as the palace faded out of sight.

When the royal princess stepped on board Pelagio's waiting ship, she was struck first by its size, then by a wave of nausea. Minutes later, the ecstasy of the unfolding adventure she always dreamed of was vomited out—half on the upper deck and half over the rail.

She glanced up at two masts looming under the full moon. Then all went black.

THAT NIGHT, Septimius did not venture out to sea but sailed within the sight of familiar shore. He took *Morning Star* out under the moon but within the hour had taken her back in again. His maiden voyage to Tiree had taught him the wisdom of being well-provisioned.

Round the cape and out of sight of the palace stood a little hut of a banished servant. The man had provided moments of freedom to the Crown Prince, on and off, during years prior. Now on the verge of tasting real adventure for the first time, Septimius went in to sup, and sleep, and gather supplies.

As the prince entered, a little monkey watched from above. When light no longer shone from underneath the hut door, a stowaway slipped aboard *Morning Star*. While Septimius snored in the bunk below his host, Babiola slept nestled amongst the tackle and extra line.

WHEN NEXT SHE AWOKE, Princess Finita found herself curled in a hammock below a creaking deck. The smell of unwashed monkey permeated the chamber. She pulled herself up to a sitting position and put her slippered feet upon the swaying floor. A dozen hammocks were strung like hers, above and beside—most of them empty. A tail hung over here and there, but the ship's motion so disoriented the princess, she had to lay back down.

A voice floated in, "She's a pretty one … "

An incoherent answer responded in turn.

"Yeah, I know she's not the queen's monkey but a royal daughter is at least good leverage. Nestorio will be pleased. Maybe not at first, but given time, he will be glad he sent a man nimble on his feet."

Finita lay down again, rolled to her side, and drew her knees up to her chest. The words "he will be pleased" sent a strange thrill through her. She smiled and fell into wondrous dreams full of colored paper and sugarplums, dolls as lifelike as human beings in gorgeous dresses. Far and wide folks came to see her dance and sing on a stage built bigger than the one promised to Babiola. Her sisters sat in the front row, calling out for an encore.

[8]

A WIDOWED QUEEN IN DESPERATE STRAITS

No boy, no girl
Now gone my man
A queen alone
An also-ran
A wing, a prayer
A ship at sea
None now remain
To comfort me

Felix, footman third class in service to King Hubert of Tiree, did not come home from his errand of great importance. A search party was never dispatched. Tiree's head steward was satisfied that the pony had returned, and Gilda Happenstance—head lady-in-waiting—was satisfied that the inconvenient baby monkey had not.

Queen Valencia asked only once for her jeweled box, home for so long to the hawthorn crown. She was reminded that it lay irretrievably at the bottom of the sea and that its loss was a small price for her honor.

After the death of his only child, King Hubert wanted to have a go at making another. But his wife put him off, quoting again and again the poet Valentius, "Everything comes to those who wait." The king had no proverb with which to answer back, so he took to other rooms—and the company of other women.

After the removal of the troublesome monkey, Queen Valencia attempted postpartum self-distraction by laboring to collect alms for orphans and widows. She found the work tiresome. She next tried a regimen of diets, intermittent fasting, and occasional prayers in the palace chapel where she lamented deeply and confessed with great honesty all of her husband's flaws. This was also tiresome.

A surprise consolation for Queen Valencia in this time of desolation was the fact that none of her husband's mistresses were found to be with child. By this Valencia was comforted. The problem of royal succession did not lay entirely at her own dainty feet.

Two and a half years after the hawthorn wreath incident, King Hubert died suddenly, choking on a giblet while laughing at his own joke. Valencia was shocked and dismayed. She had just begun to play with the idea of perhaps-maybe-might-be sending overtures his way concerning that for which he had been waiting. Being dead, her husband was no longer in a position to receive her tender propositions.

The first month of Valencia's widowhood were darker even than her postpartum doldrums. Never a mother, no longer a wife: Who was she and how did she come to this place of undoing? She noted Miss Happenstance curling her lip in disgust when she complained of loneliness, but Valencia had not the energy to confront the insubordination.

Two months after the king's burial, Valencia awoke with her first sense of purpose. Every consort intimate with the ways of King Hubert was to be categorized, i.e. given the official stamp—"out of favor." The simple act of acknowledging her genuine, well-placed anger was liberating.

One week after her liberation, Queen Valencia found the fortitude to give every "out of favor" woman three days' notice. With unprecedented royal generosity she gifted a mono-grammed bag to each in which to pack personal items. The way the gold-stitched **oFo** lay upon the leather was breathtaking.

Three days after Queen Valencia admired the mono-grammed satchels, she mustered her new-found assertiveness and ordered each consort to the seaside where they were given passes to board a commandeered schooner.

An hour after the **oFo** boarding, the queen found within her the boldness to direct the captain to sail towards shipping lanes known to be infested by lonely pirates. He could trade how he saw fit for his own expenses.

Three months to the day after the king's passing, Queen Valencia barked orders that the wing of the palace that had formerly housed the king's mistresses was to be converted into her personal library. Carpenters were given blueprints. Envoys were sent to gather spare copies and new releases from neigh-boring kingdoms. At last Queen Valencia would have what her dead husband had denied her for so long.

A third phase of Tiree's great makeover came to the queen on her way home from the expulsion of the **oFo**. Her Highness had heard a monkey cry out as the trumpets blared farewell to the schooner. By that screech something deep within her breast was re-troubled and her moment of victory nearly spoiled. In a flash, she formulated a third wave of action for total victory.

Declaring all-out war on every screaming monkey of Tiree brought a sense of mission, spurred as if by a heavenly edict. Valencia deserved happiness! And towards that rightful happiness she would eradicate all reminders of her one irreparable sorrow—a grievous misjudgment made under duress. There would be no more chattering monkeys in the trees of her realm, no more howling screeches to remind her of her childlessness.

It took weeks to accomplish, but in the end, puchin monkeys were captured and exported, mosmaret monkeys were netted and sold offshore, every vetver specimen was trapped for the valuable pelts, and the diminutive speehider were tossed into the surrounding coastal waters.

Now the queen could be happy. And she was. Except ...

Queen Valencia did not comprehend the depths of her royal solitude until a report came of a lone sailor—free-spirited and daring—weaving in and out of the neighboring islands. He seemed to answer to no one.

Valencia was fascinated.

Queen Valencia stared in the mirror. Perhaps if she had someone who truly loved her ... not as a baby-making receptacle, but as herself—her queenly heart and inherent charms. Was it too late? She wanted someone progressive, well-made, and clever. Reports of the young mystery man fit the bill. Perhaps he would be open-minded enough to see past the age difference—more than made up for by her position and wealth.

The mirror's reflection reported honestly. The queen, no longer young, was thick from stem to stern. Her eyes were small, her mouth was large, and she was not entirely hairless on her upper lip. The figure she cut was not without its advantages

—for ruling a kingdom. Her looks and bearing commanded respect, but her appearance did little to inspire love.

It is difficult to blind oneself to one's defects when they reach a certain point, even for a queen. Valencia was forced to admit that in her current condition, it would be impossible for her to please the young navigator. To do so would require beauty, or at least youth. But how? How could she change grey hairs and masculine features for an amiable figure, youthful graces, and, most importantly, an unsagging bosom?

[9]

DREAMS OF YOUTH AND MAGIC CHALK

A man, a man
She wants a man
And asks I do what no one can
Womanly wants all pass away
But yet she wants it anyway

Valencia had sworn an oath to have nothing more to do with fairies, but she was beginning to doubt there was any other course of action to achieve her desperate desires. The dreadful Sabellia had hidden herself since the fateful day of Babiola's birth. Even if summoned, she might not choose to make herself known. There was no use holding a grudge. Fickle Sabellia was a first-rate fairy with none to equal her except perhaps Marcionna of the southeast. But Valencia had read somewhere that fairies were finicky about encroaching into the territory of their sister sprites. And then there were the additional fees for mileage and travel expenses.

Books for the library had just begun to stream in. Perhaps a new arrival would provide ideas or inspiration.

Her Majesty wandered that evening towards the refurbished wing just as the workmen were released from a long day's labor. The last craftsman scurried away as she entered, hungry to go home and nervous about incurring one of the extra duties that always surrounded a queen. When Valencia entered, nothing met her but half-filled shelves under the glow of golden tapers. In and out, back and forth, she wove, dragging the fingers of her left hand through fresh sawdust while stretching out her right arm to let fingertips thump along the bound spines of the newly-arrived volumes.

In the corner farthest from the entrance, beyond the last aisle of mahogany shelves, Valencia spied a tall gilded stool beside a green candelabra. The lampstand held up the glow of six dancing flames. The stool held up a crosslegged dwarf adorned by long flowing mustaches above a clean shaven chin. His diminutive muscular body was bent over a volume covered in purple vellum and ornamented with silver clasps.

The queen approached with great respect. Dwarfs and fairies were usually at odds but were, to her knowledge, equally powerful. Perhaps upon this three-legged stool sat an answer to her prayers. Perhaps the cursed Sabellia was not needed after all.

The dwarf glanced up for a fraction of a second, but in that span Valencia knew he knew all her griefs and desires. She greeted him with words of gratitude and a quick bow, and begged he name his price and not delay.

The dwarf appreciated the queen's directness. Here was a Majesty, he sighed to himself, well-versed in the dwarfian way of abstaining from jibber-jabber. Eyes still affixed upon the page, he spoke, "Dismiss those on duty outside the hall. Lock all doors. Secure every window."

The queen obeyed.

Looking up at last to view the queen over thick readers, her guest spoke again, "My price is your first child."

"Too steep," Valencia countered without hesitation.

"First girl," came back a lightning-quick answer.

"Still too steep," said Her Majesty, a veteran of high-stakes bargaining.

"Third boy or second girl, whichever comes first. Final offer."

"Done," agreed the queen in a tone both parties knew was binding.

The dwarf stood up, balanced upon his stool, and bowed, "My name is ... "

He paused, nonplussed, as if troubled by a flash of memory.[1]

"You may call me Mr. Bunkle, Your Highness," he said at last.

"Pleased, I'm sure," said the queen with an impatient curtsey.

Mr. Bunkle pulled off his reading spectacles. Leaning in to give the queen the once-over, he concluded at once he had been had. The dowager would bear, at best, one child. He would never receive his due. Mr. Bunkle moaned inarticulately, but held his tongue.

Queen Valencia stood puzzled. Never had she encountered before such a perfect, all-encompassing poker face. She could not read him, countenance nor posture.

"What is it?" she demanded.

"I had not realized ... " said Mr. Bunkle with measured voice, "I did not know that I would be working with ... vintage wine. Your desire for youth will take some doing and clear results are not foreseeable."

Valencia nodded in comprehension, then clasped her

hands together like an excited school girl and struck a dramatic pose.

The dwarf sighed again. From an unseen pocket he pulled a braided wand of three metals intertwined—copper, nickel, and brass. From another pocket he produced a vial containing a clear greenish liquid. He seated Queen Valencia on his stool after pulling it to the middle of the grand room. She repositioned herself, palms up in expectation, ready to receive.

Mr. Bunkle pulled several books from nearby shelves and stacked them to serve as his step stool. Climbing up, he faced Valencia eye to eye, and gave firm instruction that she was to read a long underlined passage from his vellum book in a slow, inflectionless monotone. He warned her that inserting emotion or meaning, emphasis or flair, would at best necessitate her starting over. At worst, such creative liberties could turn them both into limestone statuary.

Valencia trembled and began, not daring to look up from the book placed in her lap. The dwarf hopped down and marked in chalk interlocking spirals round them both, one after another. He drew furiously as the queen droned mechanically on.

At the point of exhaustion, both his and hers, Mr. Bunkle sprang lithely back upon his platform and touched the queen's forehead three times with the wand. Next he spritzed her with flicking fingers from head to rump. The greenish liquid dissolved on contact, leaving the chamber with an odd acidic odor. Just as the smell began to the dissipate, the dwarf burst the somber mood with a loud jovial laugh, "You shall have what you ask for—youth!" he wheezed, twirling his glasses between finger and thumb. "Glorious youth, inward and outward, in fullest measure!"

Mr. Bunkle's chuckle changed all at once into a long howl. An unknown tongue[2] exploded from his lips, his little beardless body shot upward like a roman candle, and a dwarf-sized hole was blasted through the newly-built roof. Looking down, Mr. Bunkle's naked eyes saw Queen Valencia of Tiree grow tiny.

And then he disappeared.

IT WAS NOT JUST the dwarf's point of view that made Queen Valencia grow smaller. The imbued magic did not at all delay. In a flash she stood halfway between her former stature and that of her enchanter. For the first time in her adult life, she was diminutive.

The queen took no immediate notice of her transformation, for an ever-increasing fear had taken hold. All around her, blue chalk spirals spat purple flame. The fire hissed and hawked with such increasing ferocity that only a surge of primordial adrenalin gave her feet the power and energy to cross over the runic lines to make her escape. The moment she was wrapped in the arms of the cool night air, Valencia fainted dead away. She was found face-down on the dew-soaked lawn by a page the next morning.

When once again alone in her boudoir, Queen Valencia of Tiree went straightway to consult her looking-glass. There she saw, to her utmost pleasure, that her features were charming to the extreme. She did not care that from the neck up she resembled a little girl of eight or nine, including ribbons and ringlets, for below her neck all parts were those of a young woman in her prime. Matching the queen's juvenile face was her gown—a frock with short sleeves under a lace apron. The fashion of a little girl draped over an ample bosom, tapered downward towards a narrow waist, and pleated out again over spreading hips. A large smile spread across the queen's girlish face as a sudden burst of emotion for the roving sailor she had set her heart upon erupted forth.

The queen's courtiers were astonished at her change in appearance. Befuddled, they looked— as was tradition—to Prime Minister Windfall for how to respond. Windfall changed not a whit in his policy of perpetual flattery, and all the palace staff—as was also tradition—followed his lead.

In no time, the ladies of the court imitated the queen's new fashion, conforming themselves to her newly-youthful whims and manners. Lace frocks, ringlets, and short sleeves were all the rage. Persons of any import in Tiree now skipped from place to place, no matter the distance. The ladies-in-waiting fell to dressing and undressing dolls, and even the men engaged in hide-n-seek and hopscotch. Royal bakers found themselves icing double the number of cookies, tarts, and cream puffs. All the talk at dinnertime was of elaborate betrothal stories and playing house.

Gilda Happenstance put in for early retirement. Queen Valencia hardly noticed her absence.

[10]

BETTER SONGS THAN IDLE TALK

I hope that I shall never sail
Alone on seas I do not know
Who to tell but fish and whale?
Of moon above and stars below

It was several long weeks before any further word of the valiant navigator was reported to the Queen of Tiree. Youth-imbued Valencia had begun calling him Charming.

News of the sailor's notable nose did not reach the ears of Her Majesty. This omission may have been due to the inability of the royal spies to focus a telescope's eyepiece. It may be because the royal nose was always tucked behind the royal jib when a spy glass swung round in his direction. In either case, no report reached Valencia of Charming's striking profile, and this ignorance dovetailed well with the standing policy of telling her majesty only news that would please her. Still, it is doubtful that any wind of rumor could have made a dent in her enthusiasm.

AT SUNRISE, a day after disappearing from Tenpetal Hall, Septimius sailed for the first time beyond sight of home on a course that charted no quick return. After the anxiety at his own daring subsided, he noticed from the slight change in *Morning Star*'s handling, and the tip of a furry tail, that he had a stowaway. Septimius was surprised at the depth of comfort he found in Babiola's presence, but held his peace. He extended to Babiola the sanctity of her secret nestling below him in the bow, pressed by a passing worry that speaking might reawaken the awkwardness of her confessed attachment to him. But, when movement betrayed her wakefulness, she said not a word, and her reciprocal silence dispelled all his fears. The prince's mood softened, all tension fell away into the ripples along the hull, and he sank into the quiet that always accompanied his time upon the sea. Who was he to rob from anyone with a little initiative the freedom found out upon the waves?

As he ate, he let portions of his bread and fruit fall to the floorboards where he knew Babiola could reach. Nothing went to waste.

In the heat of the noonday, the morning meal fully digested, the sharpening edge of hunger returned. To distract himself from consuming his rations, Septimius began to sing a little ditty, a familiar sailing song with lyrics designed for call and response. From the first note, he expected Babiola to join in, as he had so often heard her do ashore—

Should I set sail for a beach on Tiree? O!

His stowaway did not break her silence. He tried again, this time with a long pause—

Should I set sail for a beach on Tiree? O!

All that met his ears was the lapping of waves. Babiola had left him to sing both parts as a solo. Septimius obliged her—

What care I of Tiree?
I have never set foot on its shore, O
But I find myself aching for more, O
Where you sail makes no difference
    to me.

Not even on the chorus did the monkey join in. The prince continued on alone—

Hey-dee dee,
Mis-er-able me,
Wide and long is the sea
I was loved by my mama as an itty
    bitty baby
May I die in the arms of a wrinkled
    old lady

On the second verse, much to Septimius's surprise and pleasure, Babolia's sweet small voice answered back. Her soft singing barely reached his ears over the noise of wind and wave. But if he cocked his head, he could hear it emanating up from beneath the empty seat in the bow.

S: Should I sail towards Thimbleweed,
    O!
B: Wide and long is the sea
S: Pirates there harden the soul, O
I am soft in the middle you know, O

> B: *Where you sail makes no difference*
> *to me.*

Septimius again had to sing the chorus alone, but his voice rang out a warbling baritone—

> *Hey-dee dee,*
> *Mis-er-able me,*
> *Wide and long is the sea*
> *I was loved by my mama as an itty*
> *bitty baby*
> *May I die in the arms of a wrinkled*
> *old lady*

Babiola did not hesitate to rejoin him on the third verse—

> S: *I come from Tenpetal shore, O!*
> B: *Your home has no hold on me*
> S: *Give a kiss to my mother*
> *Six sisters and no brother*
> B: *Where we sail makes no difference*
> *to me.*

As they sang with gusto together, a small island came into view. The sun was sagging towards the horizon, and the relief of sighting land pierced Septimius with joy. The taut unknown snapped into relieved euphoria, and the emboldened Crown Prince of Tenpetal picked up both the tempo and volume of the music. Babiola crawled out from her hiding place to see the cause. She sat upon the pointed bow, faced towards their destination, and sang full force in the final chorus.[1]

> *Hey-dee dee,*

> *Mis-er-able me,*
> *Deep and wide is the sea*
> *I was loved by my mama as an itty*
> > *bitty baby*
> *May I die in the arms wrinkled old lady*

The island sitting upon the horizon was larger and father away than either Septimius or Babiola had first perceived. They had long fallen silent with exhaustion when *Morning Star* wedged her bow into the beach. The two passengers crawled out up on the warm sand and curled up back-to-back to sleep beneath the stars.

11

TAKE CARE THE COMPANY YOU KEEP

Unbelieving
Eyes that see not
Ears that hear
What seems past true
There are no words
For how you find me
Do you care
How I find you?

P rince Septimius awoke the next morning to a sharp pain in his side. Glowering, he rolled over, ready to send a pageboy to the whipping block for daring to jab the royal ribs so rudely.

Squinting in the morning light, His Highness saw, instead of the paisley-patterned wallpaper of his Tenpetal bedroom, a dark silhouette cut out from a bright blue sky. Beyond the silhouette, the outline of a monkey clung high upon *Morning Star's* mast.

Septimius sat up, ran his tongue across his teeth, and spat

out a mouthful of sand. Grit and wakefulness attested to the fact he was far from his royal chamber. Through grainy lips, he posed a pressing question, "Are we on Tiree?"

The rough outline of an islander came into focus, walking stick in hand. A scruffy young man, no older than twenty, stared back at His Highness. He did not answer, but posed his own question, "Who is you?"

Septimius rose now to his feet muttering, "Who is you? ... what in the ..."

Royal ire rose up but, remembering his mother, the prince checked himself and bowed, "Good morning, sir," he said with forced courtesy. "Have I landed upon the island of Tiree?"

"Who is you?" repeated the native. "You and the nose look familiar."

Septimius drew up tall and let out a breath before replying, "I am Crown Prince Septimius of Tenpetal, exploring island to island by sail. I was wanting to reach Tiree but ... "

"Tiree is two days north. You is on Tashlin."

A commoner had interrupted a prince. But Septimius once again ignored his rudeness, glad at least for an answer.

"Thank you, good man of Tashlin," condescended his royalness. "Greetings from the House of Tenpetal, Unifier of the Radiant Three Isles ... "

"We ain't much for royalty on Tashlin," cut in the islander, "and the monkey sets back your chances at welcome even further. What is an uppity-up princeling doin' with a flea-bitten monkey anyhow?"

Septimius ignored the baiting about Babiola, and continued with royal formality, "You have my name, young man, and my rank. May I have yours in return?"

"Felix. Ex-footman. Full Citizen. The past is the past 'ere on Tashlin."

"Full Citizen," mused the prince aloud.

Babiola sat high above and said nothing, though she wished Septimius had defended her in the matter of the fleas.

"Here on Tashlin," Felix asserted again, "We minds our own matters and makes our own rules."

Septimius raised one eyebrow as Felix continued, "Tashlin folk know how well we's doin' by how long the royals—kings, queens, princes, dukes, and all that—stay out of our business."

"No royalty on the entire island?" Septimius queried, smiling at the obvious absurdity.

"None. Those that visit come in just to spy out our liberty," said Felix. "When there's no trouble to get wind of, it's easy to go unnoticed by the blue-bloods. So we settle problems fast and fair. 'Give the queen no excuse'—that's our motto. We is like children who figure how to share bread quick and quiet, lest empty-bellied pa and ma show up and snatch away the whole loaf."

Babiola dropped from *Morning Star's* mast to the deck and began rummaging around.

Septimius cleared his throat and stretched his limbs. "It sounds, sir," he said with a yawn, "like I need to re-board my little ship at once. It is unwise to remain where one is not welcome."

Felix shook his head, "Tashlin ain't pirates, mister. Yer not in danger. Tashlin will help you on towards Tiree ... anxious and eager-like. But none of us would advise ya tah keep company with a monkey—here, and more specially, there."

"No monkeys allowed on Tiree? Is the queen allergic?"

Felix roared a hearty laugh. "You hit close to true, Citizen-Prince. They 'gainst the law, hunted down to nothin'—queen's orders. Perhaps she's got the sneezes!"

Felix wheezed with delight. Septimius mirrored him and laughed alongside, slapping his thigh. "The Queen of Tiree hates monkeys. What mirth! And since no monkeys are allowed on Tashlin either, I guess the Citizens of Tashlin are allergic too?"

Felix stamped his foot and sobered, "No. We don't make monkeys welcome here on Tashlin cause we wants no royal trouble. Monkeys ain't worth it." He glanced towards the deck of *Morning Star* and called out, "Nothin' 'gainst you personal, little varmint!"

"Forgive my ignorance, Citizen Felix," said Septimius. "But what possible harm is there in one small animal?"

Felix put his hands on his hips and stretched himself tall. "Here's the state of things, Prince Long-Nose ... "

Septimius scowled.

Felix hunched and began again, "I've been on Tashlin long enough to see how things 'appen, Mr. Prince, and I'll tell you straight. You're lucky you met me first, cause not all would speak so clear-like. You will be welcome for a day, maybe two, and then sent on your well-provisioned way. But the monkey will be caged and offed."

"I am not a monkey," came a voice close to *Morning Star*.

Babiola stood as high as her small figure would allow. She wore a straw hat that had rested on Septimus for most of the voyage. A bandana was wrapped round her waist as a skirt, and she walked with a dignified gait, away from the boat towards the two men.

Felix dropped his jaw like a man who might not ever recover.

Babiola drew near, tipped her hat delicately, and made a small curtsey. "I know I might *seem* a monkey, kind host. But I am either an enchanted fairy princess, or a little woman who wears a fur coat and is in need of a shave. No one, including myself, is sure. One day, perhaps, I will wake up from this bad dream."

THE MORNING STAR WAS SECURED, her lines attached to nearby trees, and Felix stumbled forward as a guide towards the nearby town. Babiola walked straight-backed to the right of the prince while Felix maintained a position on His Highness's left.

The ex-footman was now all respect and seriousness, though he said not a word to or about Babiola. He was, in fact, trying his best to forget altogether that the bewitched creature was there at all. Babiola, conversely, was determined to drive deep into the prejudiced brain of Mr. Felix the fact that she understood every word spoken in her presence. She inserted an occasional "yes" or "no" or "you don't say" with well-timed rhythm. By these few words she quashed Felix's desperate internal campaign to convince himself that his imagination had made the monkey speak. Once or twice, she was tempted to show off her French, but thought the display might send the ex-footman back into shock.

By midway in their journey, Felix was leaning in and speaking to Septimius as one would a confidante. "A man like meself—one who served the Majesties for years and years—puts off a royal stench for what seems forever. It took me the longest to be treated as a low-down equal here on Tashlin. I still take shore patrol as often as I can, just to prove the point—all the shifts nobody wants. I tries to show a loyal lowliness. Don't want nobody to think that I think my past makes me somethin' better."

Septimius walked in silence, hands folded behind his back.

Felix prattled on, "I come from Tiree. There I was a *somebody*, trusted with important matters and pricey items. But it suits me better to live on Tashlin, to be an equal *nobody* rather than a better-than-others *somebody*."

Septimius, knowing he was a *somebody*, did not care or understand, but pretended he did with an occasional nod. He was enjoying thoroughly the waves of tension that passed through Felix each time Babiola spoke.

When Felix winked now and again at his guest, which he did any time he was particularly pleased with how he had explained or expressed some important matter, Babiola would catch his eye and wink back. Felix would then duck behind Septimius, set his face like flint forward, and quicken the pace.

THE DESTINATION VILLAGE was now in view. From the gated compound in the distance exited the figure of a middle-aged woman.

"Ah," said Felix, "The Citizen comin' our way is a fine sample of Tashlin's ways. She was once a highfalutin' lady-in-waitin', servin' Queen Valencia herself. But here on Tashlin, she lives on our outskirts. We feel sorry for her, a woman tossed out by the system she served. But 'ins' being 'outs' puts people right ... given time."

"Poor thing," whispered Babiola.

"Everyone stops stinkin' of palace eventually," said Felix aside to Prince Septimius, "but this woman was high and deep she was, high and deep."

As the woman drew nearer, Babiola suppressed an urge to leap into Septimius's arms. Something about the stranger made her monkey fur stand on end.

"Greetings, Madam Happenstance," called out Felix.

"Just Gilda, Fellow Citizen," came the brisk reply. "Are these newcomers?"

"We knew each other before in the Palace of Tiree," whispered Felix to his companions. "She does well to correct my greetin'. Shows progress."

"I found these two at the shore," called back Felix. "They're just passin' through, then on to Tiree."

"Forgive me, Citizen Felix, for questioning your wisdom," said Gilda, drawing close. "I am sure you know more than I about this matter. But is it advisable yet for a monkey to go on to Tiree?"

"She's not a monkey," said Felix firmly. "She is a little woman who wears a fur coat and is in need of a shave."

"Oh really," smirked Gilda, taking in the figure under the hat.

"Yes, I'm afraid so," said Babiola. "Either that or bewitched. No one knows. *C'est dommage.*[1]"

Gilda dropped her jaw, stepped back, and began a low bow. Then in a flash she straightened up and moved to go on. Three steps on her way, the ex-lady-in-waiting (now Full Citizen), stopped and turned towards Septimius. "Have you by chance, sir, come in by sailboat?"

"Yes ... by sail," answered Septimius with hesitation.

"A small boat, single-masted, well-made?"

Septimius nodded.

"The queen is looking for you, sir. It is basic hospitality that I tell you. Welcome to Tashlin, where the 'in' know it's good to be out, and the 'out' are happy to be in."

And with that Gilda Happenstance turned again and walked on.

Babiola watched her disappear and noted carefully the direction.

12

NOW I LAY ME DOWN TO SLEEP

And by my love and need I was undone
And by my pain was driven very far
What use to be abandoned and betrayed?
The axe upon the root it must be laid

Three days after Finita, sixth princess of the House of Tenpetal, left her palace home under the care of a pirate's ambassador, two planks instead of one stretched from the lesser ship's deck to the greater. The pirates were taking considerable care that their prize should not be lost to the waves below.

Two crewmen dressed in their best led Finita into a large cabin abutting the captain's quarters on the flagship *Landeven*. The space had been designed to be flooded with sunlight, but the windows had been boarded over. The door closed behind her and Finita was left alone with a silken sofa, a sea chest, and a small Dutch stove. Large oil paintings hung upon the walls depicting Greek goddesses in various stages of undress, some standing statuesque, others fleeing stags and wild geese. Atop the stove sat a great Chinese vase with two dragons perched upon its lid. A second room just beyond was furnished with a small armchair and a wide feather bed. The sea chest in the main room seemed to swell with the pride of its contents—lace dresses and ladies' undergarments—worth a year's wages in silver.

A tub was brought in and the young princess was instructed to wash herself. Afterward, she found a set of satin pajamas folded upon the bed and the clothes she had traveled in were missing. The pajama shirt and trousers fit her small frame, if she rolled the cuffs of both arms and legs twice. Finita liked the cloth of bright iridescent green. Her enjoyment increased when she found it matched one of several weaves in the thick carpet under her bare feet. If only her sisters could see what was now hers! Gone were her days of being tucked into the bed of her childhood, draped in a cotton gown. Her missing clothes did not trouble her in the least for she was used to royal garments disappearing and reappearing, laundered and pressed.

What splendor awaits me! Finita thought, quivering in anticipation.

A distant parrot on a distant shoulder seemed to cry, "Take care! Take care!"

She shivered hearing it, fearing she would some how let all that was unfolding before her slip away like a bewildering, wonderful dream.

Peeking through the slats in her windows, the princess saw the troop of monkeys she had traveled with dancing about the deck, swinging round the main mast, snatching a morsel here and there from a passing sailor. Finita thought of Babiola and how this bright future could have been hers, had she but chosen it.

The creaking door cause her to turn. A tray was brought in

by an old man hobbling on a stump. He said not a word past "your majesty," bowed low, and left. Whether the fare was below or above her royal palate, Finita did not know. She ate all but tasted nothing, for she could only think—what is going to happen next?!

The tapers were burning low. Finita did not notice that as she slipped off to sleep, someone slipped in to blow them out one by one. Neither did she notice, before the room was quite dark, her cover lifted for inspecting eyes to scan her from head to heel.

THREE DAYS after Septimius and Babiola left Tenpetal, makeshift beds were laid down in the small house of Felix Full Citizen. Their host had no intention of sharing a room with what might be a monkey, so Babiola's pallet was set up in the adjoining kitchen.

Though Felix's rectangular hut was well-made, there was nothing but bare walls and basic necessities. One door opened into the main room where a bed skulked in the corner, unmade. The only window the house possessed was carved out of the back wall of the kitchen. Shutters, designed to allow a cross breeze to drive out smoke from the wood-burning stove, sagged across the pane-less opening. Thick drapes made to separate the kitchen from the main room huddled, clutching themselves against the back wall. They were rarely closed but Felix pulled them across now and hoped the monkey would exit behind them on her own. The vermin chose instead to dart in and out of her keeper's shadow.

The single chair in the main room was offered to the prince. Felix pulled up an apple crate for himself and a packing case to act as table. He snatched a sheet from his creaky bed frame to serve as a table cloth. Three vessels were taken from the single kitchen cupboard: two tin cups and one wooden bowl. From these, the three travelers supped. Emptied and wiped clean, the same receptacles served rain water collected from a barrel just outside the entrance.

What opulence I once thought was standard fare, thought Babiola.

Is this how all commoners live, or is this squalor the byproduct of a string of bad choices? wondered Septimius to himself as new thoughts came crowding.

Both guests sat without word in their bewilderment.

While Septimius attempted polite conversation, Babiola's eyes roved every crevice. In an alcove in the west corner, where a coat closet might be built (had Felix found the will) sat a pile of odds and ends. Babiola noted a moth-eaten overcoat, crumpled brown paper, tangled twine, candle stubs, and a curious box.

The box was exquisite. It did not belong. Light dancing in from the setting sun outside caused a glimmer on its surface, as from gold and diamonds.

Felix rose and closed the front (and only) door, working to steady his breath, hoping his guests had not seen. In the dimness, he could no longer attempt to read their faces. Had they seen? Could they count the missing jewels, pried off one by one? Would he have to tell why he, so late in coming, was chosen by Tashlin to pay the pirates for protection, month after befuddling month? How could he explain how he came to shoulder the burden of buying freedom—freedom that allowed the islanders to walk where they pleased and assign for themselves their own chosen work? What explanation did he owe to anyone, especially these two?

The fire burned low, the sun sank, and the moon shone half-strength. Soft starlight crept under the door and through the kitchen shutters, but the wind was too cool now to reopen either portal.

Septimius yawned and stretched out on his pallet. Felix paced, struggling with whether he should offer the Crown Prince his bed. His Majesty's rattling snore settled the quandary. A forceful wind whistled in and out of the mighty nostrils, and with it, a flash of memory rushed through the ex-footman's addled brain. Felix turned to where the monkey had last stood, but she had gone beyond the curtain and was out of sight.

The prince, the box, and the monkey converged in the footman's mind.

The kitchen was quite dark but Babiola felt inspecting eyes peer round the edge of the drapes, scanning her from head to heel as she lay down upon the cobblestones. She turned her back to the intruding gaze and curled up before warm coals nestled at the bottom of the stove.

When he at last crawled up onto his creaking bed, Felix could not sleep. The flash of sunlight on the box had brought the slow-in-coming connections. The man snoring at the foot of his bed owned the same pair of arms into which he had lain the baby monkey found locked within the jeweled chest so long ago.

The monkey could speak. He, Felix ex-footman Full Citizen, had chosen not to drown an enchanted beast! Only good could come from the wisdom of such a self-controlled decision. But what good? Last month he had paid the dread pirate, Nestorio, de facto emperor of the Rogasian Archipelago, what was due him.

Now he recalled that Nestorio's men had spoken of a magic monkey ... that their chief was obsessed ...

What were the chances of two magic monkeys in all the wide Rogasian Sea? Sleeping before his stove might be the answer to the burning question troubling his heart for months now—what would happen when there were no more diamonds left to pry loose?

[13]

HUMAN HANDS AND MONKEY PAWS

Stretched out before the life-long wait
With none to look and validate
Cares unwind from tight-wound fret
Desire sighs, off-flies regret
When all is lost, no need to grasp
When food is scarce, no need to fast

Minutes after sunrise, whatever dreams and plans floated through Felix's sleep were shattered by a banging at the door.

Before opening his eyes, Felix recognized voices from every corner of the island surrounding his house. Both young and old called out, "Where is the prince and monkey who came to you yesterday? Bring them out to us, so we might rid Tashlin of their odious presence."

Felix jumped up, and in two hops stood upon his stoop with the door shut tight behind him, "No, my Fellow Citizens. Don't be hasty. I was 'bout to feed'em and send'em on. Lemme bring the monkey out to show you ... you'll understand my waitin'. There's no disloyalty, please believe! But don't do nothin' rash to the royal. He understands our ways and he's ready to go."

"Get out of our way!" voices in the mob screamed.

"This fellow is foreign royalty and you still love to kiss their arses!!"

"You ain't no Citizen!"

"News of Prince Big Nose has already reached the lustful Queen of Tiree! Our spies tell us she sails with the wind to her back."

Felix's eyes threaded through the crowd, seeking an understanding face. He knew each man by name, but suddenly found no friend. The swarm pressed him back against his front door, quivering on its hinges, threatening to break.

"If her majesty makes land," shrieked a cutting voice, "we shall have no peace or freedom for a generation!"

"Wait till she sees her lover boy has a monkey!"

In a hair's breadth of silence, a soft feminine inflection pierced through the chaos. The mass of men took a collective step back as the door opened, sending Felix reeling upon the threshold with a thump. Framed in the doorway stood Babiola. A piece of a frayed blanket was wrapped her like a toga. Her handkerchief tied round it as a sash was affixed with an ornamental bow.[1] Under the straw hat she had added Felix's reading glasses, lenses popped free, giving her the look of a dignified spinster ready for her morning stroll.

The collective jaw of the angry crowd dropped as Babiola addressed them, "Kind sirs, I hear your concerns. If you will let me pass through I will cause you no more trouble. Bid me *adieu*. I am on my way, and I promise you will see me no more."

A heavy silence fell. The mob parted. Babiola walked out on the path provided, like a starlet on the red carpet among adoring fans.

Babiola's insides clawed at her. Apelike instinct screamed to scamper on all fours, to shimmy up the nearest tree, to leap from branch to branch where she could screech at those below in passionate defiance. But somehow, counteracting all animal impulse, was an intense weight of knowing. Babiola knew that to be a lady was her only path to freedom.

Passing through the midst of them, she went on her way.

The multitude, as one man, turned from the hut of Felix ex-footman and watched the figure of a monkey-lady saunter towards the trees. Her gait was neither slow nor fast. Just steady.

"*Adieu!*" came a call from one of the youngest. He was quickly cuffed and corrected, "Curb your tongue, Nave! No French here! That's the speech of royal bastards."

Three others followed up with a stair-stepped chorus, "Goodbye! Goodbye! Goodbye!" showing that Tashlin citizenry knew how parting was done.

Babiola lifted the back of her paw in salute, but walked on without turning.

"God Bless!" called another, then another, then another.

And then she was gone, not a soul noting her direction, all feeling a collective sense of nebulous satisfying calm.

Never had Septimius, Crown Prince of the Tenpetal Isles, moved so quickly. He had very little to gather for he had slept in his clothes. Boots in hand, he squeezed his lanky body out through the kitchen window—badly bruising his nose—and flew in the direction of *Morning Star*.

The little boat seemed to be watching and waiting. Her sail was set, her hull unbeached. Floating free she pointed northward. Septimius took twelve splashing strides, threw himself over her port side, and landed with a thud. Cautiously he glance behind him shoreward, only his forehead and eyes peeping up over the rail. Not a soul had pursued.

Only when Tashlin disappeared in *Morning Star's* wake, did Septimius think at last to put his boots back on his badly bruised feet. Only when his boots were laced tight and his shirt tucked in did it dawn on the prince that he sailed away alone.

He had left Babiola behind.

That night under the waning moon, Crown Prince Septimius set his anchor, put his face in his hands, and wept. Like the undeniable depths below, there was no reframing the fact that he had saved his own skin and forgotten his friend.

At last, though his heart felt no lighter for the shedding of them, there were no more tears. Wiping his face, Septimius determined he would displace his sorrowful shame with grim determination. At first light, he would turn back.

But second chances are too often the stuff of imagination. The Crown Prince of Tenpetal awoke from too few hours' sleep to find himself surround by boats sent by Queen Valencia of Tiree. She had given orders for her happily-ever-after to be towed straight to shore, into her waiting arms.[2]

Out of sight of Felix's house, when the din of the crowd had shrunk to silence, Babiola continued to walk upright. Above were branches, below were roots and—traveling in between— she felt the island was striving to tell her something, something about herself, something true. She had every intention of arriving at her destination with the stealth of an animal— peering and peeking, scenting and honing. But the closer she came to arriving, the more animal instinct faded into extinc- tion. With each step she felt less monkeyish.

Two hind feet took her to the door of a cottage deep in the woods. It stood plain and rectangular, much like Felix's, but even less welcoming. She raised her hand to knock, but could not follow through.

The door opened anyway.

Gilda Happenstance, in a single motion, beckoned her guest inward and propped the door open with a small crate. Babiola was glad to hear no click of a latch behind her. She had come on her own, and might feel a need to leave on her own, without warning.

Gilda took Babiola's hat, hung it on a peg, pulled out a second bowl and split the about-to-be-eaten breakfast between them. Babiola ate, but tasted nothing. The hostess did not eat, but stared down at her portion. The fresh morning air came in to keep them company but left just a quickly. When at last Gilda spoke, she began like a supplicant mid-confession, "I was just doing my duty, Your Highness. It's not mine to make choices and moralize. I hope you won't hold it against me now that I've been put out too."

Babiola knitted her brow in confusion. The woman's words were nonsensical, but it was the servile manner in which she spoke that was most befuddling. How was she, a little monkey, being treated as a grown woman's superior? Once or twice, Septimius had treated her like an almost-equal. And Finita had acted at times like an almost-friend. Gilda's inflection and posture communicated neither equality nor friendship, but a plea for mercy.

Gilda stopped mid-sentence, noting her visitor's perplexed silence. "Did Felix tell you nothing? Has the idiot forgotten or does he just claim no remembrance? He has indeed perfected a selective recollection."

Babiola held her tongue.

"Speak to me, Princess, please speak," continued Gilda, again almost begging, "Or I will fall apart and become a fool."

"Why do you call me Princess?" said Babiola. "I smell of royalty only because I lived among them as a pet."

"Not so, not so," whispered Gilda, "you are so much more ... *so much more.*"

"Living alone in the woods has made you part witch, madam," said Babiola, growing irritated.

"Perhaps so, perhaps so," came a hiss, barely audible.

"Stop your murmuring!" growled the monkey-princess.

Gilda began to moan. "I who did the tossing am now tossed out."

"Are you able," said Babiola, "to speak in something other than riddles?"

"Why yes, your majesty!" said Gilda. "I can sing."

And before Babiola bade her to sing or keep silent, Gilda Happenstance belted out a long-pent-up tune—

> *Who am I to speak of place*
> *Though I know who and what you are*
> *'Tween monkeys and the human race*
> *Is the gap so wide and far?*
> *The princely coward has your heart*
> *I know not why but it is so*
> *With you, your mother chose to part*
> *But will she ever let him go?*
> *Sixth sister now with buccaneers*
> *Caged wherein you should have gone*
> *You ran with wisdom, much to fear*
> *On her it just begins to dawn*

Gilda fell back to moaning, as if the remaining verses were best forgotten.

Babiola drew close and took her turn at whispering. "It seems to me you want me to die from wondering," she hissed in Gilda's ear.

Gilda stared forward, unable to look her guest in the eye, but still she gave answer. "I should have killed you myself at the beginning. But now your tale has come too far and I find it much more gratifying to watch it unfold. You may die yet."

"Everyone dies," said Babiola. "But how did my tale move to center stage? When did I become a main character? I am no conquerer. I just survive."

"That you live is victory, Princess," Gilda cackled. "You'll see. You'll know."

Babiola stepped upon a chair on tiptoe, straining to reach to her fullest stature, and commanded the crowing ex-lady-in-waiting, "Restrain your madness, woman! Speak plainly. Or more will fall upon you than falling apart!"

Mistress Happenstance obeyed. "You were born a princess of Tiree. I am the handmaid who pronounced your doom."

With these truncated sentences, Gilda double over in laughter.

Babiola took up a serving spoon and broke it over her head.

Gilda straightened and continued her disjointed recitation. "Your place among the pirates was taken by Princess Finita. There won't be anything royal left about her when they're done."

Gilda began again her cackling and this time Babiola used a broom handle.

Sobered once more, the old maid spat, "Your mother thinks she has found the fountain of youth and wants to bed Septimius, while I play the part of an old witch deep in the woods. Wait till she sees his nose!"

Gilda took a deep breath, smiled strangely, and added, "A

fine tangle. Make sense of it if you can. Piece it together if you dare."

Miss Happenstance smiled, opened her mouth to speak, and crowned her performance of jumbled half-revelations by fainting dead away.

The fragmented influx of information crashed against Babiola in waves: sorrow, loss, and then an odd strength—strength that came from knowing. She now had words for what she had long been aware of, but could not name.

The little princess-monkey stepped over the unmoving body of her mother's former maidservant, opened every closet and cupboard and larder, and helped herself to the contents. She was ravenous and ate, not as a scavenging monkey, but as a princess who had come a step closer to her birthright. Princess Babiola, heir-apparent to the kingdom of Tiree, ate until she was satisfied. Afterward, she wiped the corners of her mouth on a checkered dishrag, neatly folded her toga, and went to bathe hands, feet, and head in the nearby spring.

HIGH-BORN TEARS AND DRUNK GUFFAWS

The faults of others, too often
have dominion over me.
To my own faults
Sorrow makes me blind
'All is mercy! All is mercy!'
call the billows of the sea
A knot untangled
only over time

Queen Valencia was giddy when she received the news that her flagship *Quimpus* had docked with Prince Charming in tow. She was unable to eat her usual lunch and left the pastries untouched. Filled with sweet cream, dog-shaped eclairs sculpted into prancing poodles drooped and melted, waiting unappreciated upon the table.

The charming Septimius was met at the docks and escorted to a nearby inn where proper attire and accoutrements awaited him. The queen intended for her heartthrob to be paraded through town with great pageantry. Septimius, for all the tugging and pulling in directions beyond his control, was comforted somewhat to be treated like royalty again. The relief of having his station properly recognized gave him the grace to weather all whispers, slights, and snickers regarding his nose. Why did the nasal commentary increase the further he traveled from home?

No matter.

So a queen loved him ... a lonely queen ... and there was no Tireenian heir ... hmm ... What would his father have him do? Perhaps, if Tenpetal and Tiree were one, Tashlin's anti-royal sentiment could be brought to heel. It felt princely to engage in politics again, especially here, far out from under his father's shadow.

Once washed, Septimius lay back on his bed as servants arrived and dressed him. Their ministrations in no way intruded into the machinations of his mind. If Tiree were his, Tashlin could be properly governed. The addition of two large islands would make Tenpetal a force to reckon with, a power that did not kowtow to pirates!

Septimius had long surmised that Tenpetal's suffering found all its roots in Nestorio's flotilla of crime, the bane of the archipelago. The wicked pirate was the reason for the quashed overprotected lives of his sisters, responsible for the political necessity of Babiola's betrayal, and, most sinful of all, at the root of his father the king's constant (though well-hidden) fear.

Who was this queen of Tiree? How old was she? Was she suited to him in height and manners? How far might he stretch his tastes for the greater good?

WHILE SEPTIMIUS WAS BEING BATHED, redressed, re-coiffed, and re-shod, Queen Valencia was twirling through the spacious halls of her palace. Whimsical and flighty, her outward show matched her inner emotions. The happiest moment of her life had at last arrived, and she began to babble to any who stood near all about her Charming. She, the young and beautiful queen, in view of all her citizens, would run to meet him with wide open arms. The glorious answer to all her prayers would make his way through her city streets as young and old, rich and poor came out to participate in her joy.

Valencia's intention to make public display of her passions appalled the household staff. A collective attempt, using all powers of persuasion, was brought to bear upon the queen, begging her to go no further than the stairs in the palace entrance. Even this far was contrary to generations of established etiquette.

Valencia could not (would not) hear anything counter to her romantic fantasies until a clever washerwoman offered up a delirious distraction. The old woman produced by subtle suggestion a dramatic mental image: an awe-inspiring theatrical descent down the grand staircase wearing an ever-lengthening train. A step at time beautiful Valencia would descend before an enthralled Prince Charming.

Valencia was captivated.

During her eighth run-through in the third-to-last dress rehearsal, Queen Valencia became entangled in her pink sequined gown and fell. The tumble was quite turbulent, and, although Her majesty's hands saved her head, her nose was grazed and several fingernails chipped. Valencia, screeching in fright, was carried to her chamber where her face was bathed with lavender water, and smelling salts were wafted under her delicate nostrils. The staff despaired of her ever gaining composure until news of the prince's early arrival reached the chamber. Prince Septimius Charming himself stood even now, waiting to see her at the foot of stairs in the great hall.

Holding a stuffed toy for courage, Valencia approached the banister once more. Septimius glanced up. Into his line of vision came a shapely queen in ringlets wearing pink ruffled taffeta. With her right hand she twirled a lock at her temple and with her left she clutched an overstuffed teddy bear.

Septimius burst into a violent fit of laughter. So taken by hilarity was the Crown Prince of Tenpetal that he was obliged to leave the vestibule for fresh air. As he stumbled, doubled over, out into the adjoining garden, Queen Valencia watched him depart and began to cry.

"Charming, Charming, I want my Charming!"

Only the intervention of the nearby washerwoman kept her from regressing into thumb sucking.

SEPTIMIUS, hearing and fearing the queen's continuing pleas, slipped away out through a back garden gate. As he distanced himself from the palace, he was relieved to find himself tailed by no more than a slightly built pageboy. The boy, by his pace and manner, seemed to be following out of curiosity, as if he found the whole situation fascinating.

As they ambled down the hill and away, Septimius nodded to his follower. The boy nodded back.

"Is she insane, boy?" Septimius said.

The boy smiled a wide grin and answered, "Only recently, Prince Charming, Sir."

"Charming? Is that what she calls me?" questioned Septimius, motioning for the boy to walk close by.

"Prince Charming is how *all* of us are instructed to address you, sir."

Septimius snorted then asked, "And how should I address you, boy?"

"Britt will do, sir. Thanks for asking."

Both traveled quietly for a long pace over the smooth cobblestones to an area where the houses grew thick and ramshackled. A hard turn brought them to an alley of close-knit shops. The prince paused, realizing he was traveling towards an unknown destination, and looked down to Britt for any hint of guidance.

Britt stared up, "No one ever mentioned your nose, sir."

"And I would be obliged," answered Septimius, "if you did not either."

Britt's face fell in disappointment but, still beholden that a prince had learned his name, led Septimius to a tavern he knew to be hospitable. It stood in a less desirable part of town, but Britt knew that here, none of the Queen's lackeys lurked. The tavern also had rooms to rent above, and Britt was the kind of page that thought ahead.

Upon entry, Britt drew aside the proprietress who, without hesitation, showed her guest to a comfortable seat in the corner. The lad then turned to leave. Septimius motioned for him to stay.

"Can't, my lord, they'll be missing me. But don't fret, sir. You're in good hands. Most here hope you will restore the queen's dignity, tame her desires and all. Even those far from the palace are beginning to grow weary of living under a tyrant-child."

With that, he, and his little voice of wisdom, were gone.

For the first half hour, the tavern left Septimius to eat and drink and think in peace. He pondered how to reach the *Morning Star*, wondered whether her rigging had been put under lock and key, and did his best to give no thought to either the shameful leaving of Babiola or the oddness of the queen.

Then came the sniggering and clandestine pointing from other tables.

"Nose-envy," thought Septimius, for not a man in the tavern had half his claim to size.

He motioned to the proprietress, asking, "Madam, have the goodness to give me something more to eat. And please tell me, have I done anything to offend your other guests?"

"More food's on the way, sir," answered the matron, adding with a whisper and a wink, "Don't mind them, sir. Even though your nose is ... how shall I put it ... notable. We all have high and happy hopes you can satisfy the passions of her majesty."

Septimius ate, but took no pleasure in the hearty meal, for it was difficult to not hear the snickers and jokes floating through the air at his expense.

"It's a good nose, there's just too much of it," came a statement from a far corner, loud enough to be heard and soft enough to feign privacy.

"It is something, to be sure, but a wife's wagging tongue is more insufferable than a man's large nose, even one such as that."

The hour grew later and lips loosened further. At last, a well-sopped patron stood on his chair in mock complaint, "Prince Charming! Move a little, I'm beggin' ya. Your nose makes so large a shadow that it prevents me from seein' what's on my plate."

All the diners and drinkers roared.

Septimius retired upstairs in silence, his plate and cup sent up after.

[15]

AT LAST PRINCE CHARMING BENDS
TO KISS

Blame all my troubles on ills that life dishes
Defects and sins,
Acknowledge them? No
Till flaws become obstacles to my best wishes
I leave them to fester,
I leave them to grow

When the man of her dreams did not return, Queen Valencia became inconsolable. In vain the palace staff tried to calm her, but her tantrumming only increased. All were weary and near their wits' end. The guest prince had escaped out from under the absurdity of their daily toil. His fresh eyes brought to focus the insufferable reality: the queen was impossible and not likely ever to improve. Groom and page, cook and bootblack, even those who liked her majesty best lost hope.

Whispers of a dethroning whirled throughout the royal estate. Hints of insurrection wafted into the orbit of the chief politician, and Prime Minister Windfall was quick to smell the change.

The only spot undisturbed by rumor and intrigue was a certain corner tucked away in the queen's newly built but now rarely visited library. Finding such choice real estate unoccupied, a certain dwarf re-took up old habits. Valencia might have lost her interest in books since her metamorphosis, but Mr. Bunkle had not, even though he knew such action broke with magician guild protocol. Volume twenty-seven, section twelve, paragraph three:

> Any who deigns to execute impactful enchantments upon a sovereign(s) may do so only with the express permission of said sovereign(s) and within the clearly defined domain of the enchantee(s). After the application of agreed-upon enchantment(s), a practitioner must exit the official territory of enchantee(s), never to return.

The "never to return" was usually interpreted by the guild as a hiatus of two generations minimum, but Mr. Bunkle, unable to resist the beauty of row after row of unbroken spines, set even this liberality aside. What did the guild care about about triflings on faraway Tiree?

The dwarf sat combing through an ordinary book[1] on what he believed to be an ordinary day, when, to his great displeasure, an unordinary conversation interrupted his focused perusal. Tucked in the northwest corner, Minister Windfall and the chief steward stood conniving and contriving. Neither man was aware that every mutinous whisper bounced upon the vaulted ceiling and into the ears of the dwarf.

Mr. Bunkle, still smarting from the loss of payment, balked at the idea of losing his peaceful retreat as well. The comfort of her majesty's books was the only solace that soothed his smarting loss of a royal baby. A change of dynasty was out of the question. There was nothing for him to do but disenchant the queen.

The dwarf sighed at the inconvenience, even though the magic required at this juncture was child's play.[2] All Mr. Bunkle needed was a bottle of Valencia's tears (always in supply, easy to collect), the right phraseology (memorized in grammar school), and a five-minute wafting of burning oleander in a brass censer (both were in Mr. Bunkle's ever-deepening pockets).

That night near midnight, without a single hiccup, the queen was returned to her old normal self. Everyone but Valencia sighed in collective relief.

The next morning, at the sight of her natural face in the looking glass, Queen Valencia thought of stabbing herself in despair. Whether she had the form of an old fool or a young halfwit, her heart longed for the seafaring prince. If her youthfulness had not captured Charming, how would the face of a matron serve her cherished pursuit any better? All was hopeless.

So deep was Valencia's languor that palace staff began to pity her. They judged that she had suffered enough from childlessness and widowhood, and should now be forgiven her escapade in the fountain of youth.

Prime Minister Windfall labored at every turn to reestablish his loyalty. To prove his renewed fidelity he dedicated himself to the task discovering the whereabouts of Prince Charming. Windfall sent no lackey, but searched in person, high and low until at last, he found the inn where Septimius slept. Once behind closed doors, Windfall fell to begging him to agree to a second interview with his queen.

Septimius acquiesced, not because he had any desire to know her majesty better but because the Prime Minister showed the utmost self-control concerning his nose (a subject about which Septimius was growing quite sore). Not once did Windfall take a second look at the hood ornament upon the otherwise lovely face, and Septimius was washed over in gratitude.

"You will find our queen quite changed, sir," said Windfall, as they rode in a closed carriage towards the palace.

"I should hope so," replied Septimius.

"An awful spell has been undone, Your Highness, but there may still be hindrances … "

"Is that not for me to judge, Mr. Windfall?"

"Has anyone mentioned her age, your majesty?" continued Windfall with some hesitancy. "What you glimpsed before is much changed."

"Is that not for me to judge, Mr. Windfall?" repeated the Crown Prince of Tenpetal. He waved his hand for silence, and the Prime Minister of Tiree obeyed.

THE MEETING in Queen Valencia's sitting room was far from straightforward.

It took some time for Prince Septimius to realize that the dowager seated before him was indeed the before-seen infatuated, fit-throwing young female. This was no precursor, some matronly warmup act. Before him was not the queen's chaperone, but the queen herself, the woman who intended to make him her lover. How could she be the same foolish child-queen who greeted him earlier?

Queen Valencia began to giggle.

Septimius stared at her puzzled.

"Did you pick that nose?" she tittered.

Septimius grew red.

"We all overlook our noses," she guffawed, holding her sides, "but everyone must overlook yours!"

Now the queen was crying, "What do you call a nose not attached to a body?"

"I'm sure I do not know," answered Septimius stiffly.

"Nobody knows!" screamed the queen merrily, "Get it? Nobody's nose!"

Septimius stood, but did not know where to go, or how to exit. He faced the old matron and attempted to be formal, "I am, your majesty, Prince Septimius, heir to the Tenpetal Islands. Can you not at least rise and greet me, sovereign to sovereign?"

Valencia did not hear. She was hunched over, wheezing.

Septimius paced now liked a caged animal, "I must beg my leave of you, your highness. I am not sure why I was summoned. Surely you have better forms of entertainment than for foreign princes to be ill-used."

With this, the queen sobered enough to catch her breath, rise, and curtsey. Still, she could not look directly into her would-be lover's face. The whole situation, not just his nose, had grown ridiculous.

Wiping her eyes, the queen tried to regain a modicum of royal dignity. "I must beg your pardon, Prince. I have been a young fool and an old fool, and you have been grossly inconvenienced. Let us find a way to end this interview and part on amicable terms."

"Yes, your majesty," Septimius said, taking a seat. "Tenpetal and Tiree have never been at odds; it would be a shame to have a rupture now."

"Let us do better than a lack of acrimony," said the queen, smiling. "Let us make the islands allies."

"Excellent, your majesty. This line of discourse is to my

liking," answered the prince, relaxing into politics. "How do you propose we move forward?"

"Simply," said the queen. "You help me regain my honor as a woman and I, since I have no offspring, will write you into my will."

"It is my duty to restore a queen's honor if it be in my power," said Septimius, trying to take in the shock of what was set before him all the while attempting to discern any double meaning in Valencia's words.

"All I ask on your part," continued the queen, "is a private peck and a public show."

"Please be specific," said Septimius. "It has been a strange few days and I would deeply appreciate if your meaning were unambiguous."

"You will become the official heir of Tiree," she answered with more clarity than Septimius could have ever dreamed. "It will serve my conniving two-faced prime minster right. I am not just willing to authorize the scheme, I am eager to make it binding."

Prince Septimius nodded dumbly. Negotiating in clear-cut terms had been included nowhere in his political education. During his semester studying inter-kingdom affairs, he had received a merit badge in obfuscation, a second prize in double-speak, but nothing in his training prepared him for conditions a child could understand.

"All I ask is that you lay my little-girl dreams to rest," said Queen Valencia. "A single kiss from Prince Charming—at this hour, in this very chamber—and I will consider the affection as down payment on all of Tiree."

"My pleasure, my lady," said Septimius, hardly believing what he heard. "But understand I have suffered humiliation also. After the kiss, may I leave this very hour to board *Morning Star*? May I have your blessing to sail at once?"

"This evening perhaps, tomorrow morning more likely, dear Septimius, for I desire a parade in which we travel arm in arm down to the docks to see you off."

"Agreed," said the prince gruffly. "Let's get on with it."

"Watch your haste, young man. I am in good health and will not die tomorrow. The public show must continue any time our paths happen to cross in the future. You will not mention any indignities you have witnessed, but treat me with the respect due a benefactress."

Septimius could not help but furrow his brow, but in a blink recovered his placid countenance.

Valencia said, "I am already planning an island tour including your home of Tenpetal." Then she added with a wink, "But don't fret, my prince. There I will kiss only your mother and father. You owe me but the one."

Septimius nodded, stood, and bowed.

"Is it not right, young prince, that I see the homeland of my heir?"

"Yes, your majesty."

"Come kiss me then, you ridiculous suitor."

Septimius exhaled, approached the queen with quiet grace, bending to give what was required of him.

And could not.

The largeness of his nose would not let him. His lips could reach neither cheek nor waiting lips. The bridge of his oversized proboscis prevented all contact.

The queen, who had closed her eyes to receive, now opened them and began to giggle again.

Septimius tried once more from the opposite angle.

No use.

Valencia chortled, "Don't worry, my boy [hiccup-gasp]. I will still keep my end of the bargain. You tried ... [chortle-giggle]."

Septimius backed from the room as the queen fell into fresh hysterics. "A nose by any other name would still smell as sweet!"

The Crown Prince of Tenpetal wanted to run, just as fast and as hard as when he had fled from the house of Felix ex-footman. But he did not. He walked with quiet dignity out of the palace, down the hill, through the town, and out upon the pier. Once there, he untied the *Morning Star* and shoved off.

[16]

REGAL PRIDE REDUCED TO MIST

Some will hate that I am gone
Some relieved that I should flee
I hope at least, my friend, you know
I did not freely choose to go
Yet to stay
Would make a lesser me

Septimius found sailing away from Tiree more difficult than arriving. The prevailing currents made a three-day trip north into a six-day trip south. Ocean water beat so strongly against *Morning Star's* prow that, if the wind had not been her captain's ally, she might never have reached Tashlin. Septimius was determined to retrieve Babiola and undo his cowardice, but his low spirits and bruised ego would have been no match for doldrums.

Septimius gave no consideration to the unpredictability of the islanders, nor to the impression his newly-tailored finery might make. He only thought of his friend and whether or not she would come down to the beach to meet him.

When *Morning Star's* nose once more nuzzled the soft sands of Tashlin, Babiola was nowhere in view. The beach was empty. His monkey brought no greeting, but up the shore and beyond the tree line awaited a beating he had never before imagined. Several dozen men, glowering and hostile, had seen the slow-moving sail and conspired to provide a painful welcome. Septimius's assailants inflicted, in great rapidity, bruises, scrapes, and cuts. They gifted the prince with two black eyes, a chipped tooth, and a broken nose.

His Highness awoke from unconsciousness to find himself locked in a hut near the center of one of several ragtag villages. Voices outside argued on and on about how best to kill royalty and what kind of story should be concocted to excuse it.

Septimius could barely see through swollen slits and spent all day and most of the night in a state of semi-wakefulness. In an exhausted fog, he half-dreamt of a monkey crawling through a loosened set of tiles just above him on the roof. With the monkey came a jug of water and a whispered command to drink. There was the jingling of keys and the turning of a lock. A furry hand took his and the same whisper ordered him to come.

In perfect obedience Septimius walked out under a moon-less sky. Miles later, he collapsed onto the deck of the *Morning Star* with no spirit left to wonder at her half-stripped condition. The natives would be back at sunrise to finish her off, he supposed. Still thinking he walked within a dream, he fell into untroubled slumber upon the rocking waves.

WHEN SEPTIMIUS AWOKE, his boat was traveling upon the strong current northward with no furling sail or Tenpetal ensign flittering above. Babiola was curled up in a tight ball in the crook of his arm, breathing deeply. She wore neither hat nor bandana nor toga. Her dark fur glistened in the sunrise. She looked to him like one who dreamed happily of being a nobody as she slept in deep contentment next to the tattered prince of nothing.

Both passengers sat up and stretched, noting the empty horizon. Septimius dragged his fingers overboard to get a sense of his pitiful boat's sail-less speed. He could find nothing to gauge a change of position at any surrounding compass point, in the clear blue sky above, or down in the depths below. Looking out through blackened puffy eyes, he made a halfway-peace with his helplessness. Laying back down next to his companion he whispered, "Thank you. I came back to save you, and you saved me."

Babiola smiled a small smile and looked away, but the prince went on, "You, so magnificently human, and I, the cowering animal. How have you been since I abandoned you?"

"Acting human saved me from the mob," answered Babiola. "Being a monkey allowed me my own escape and to aid in yours."

"Felix was your jailer?"

"Not Felix, poor lout," Babiola yawned. "Do you recall meeting a certain Citizen Gilda?"

Septimius drummed his temples and shifted to *Morning Star's* stern. "Yes ... the strange woman who passed us our first day on Tashlin? Felix called her Madam Happenstance, I believe."

Babiola nodded. "When the mob came, I retreated to her hut, but I am afraid I reminded her of past sins. She invited me in as a guest. But the more human I behaved, the more pathetic her hospitality became."

Babiola paused to laugh—part monkey squeak, part human joviality—then went on, "When I went to bathe, she burned my clothes. If you can call what I dressed myself in clothes."

"So, Happenstance is tied to your past?" said the prince, perplexed.

"It seems she knows a great deal about *both* of us."

"What did she say?" said Septimius, his voice rising. "What did you learn?"

Babiola remembered the mocking tune when her hostess sang, but did not choose to sing it for her friend. The *Morning Star* was only fit for happy tunes.

"She spoke for hours on the subtle but undeniable differences between monkeys and humans," Babiola said, voice trailing off. "Perhaps she was referring only to my strange case though ... " Monkey eyes penetrated the Prince of Tenpetal with an intensity that made Septimius avert his gaze.

When Babiola began again, a chattering cadence eclipsed her mellow tone, "Gilda also spoke of the Queen of Tiree and her intense attachment to you."

"Undeniably accurate there," Septimius granted without hesitation.

"So you've been to Tiree?"

"And back again. It is a fun place to visit, but I could not stay."

Babiola rested her chin upon her paws and stared. Septimius gripped the broken tiller though steering was pointless. She required his tale and there was no escape.

Septimius laid out all that had happened since he ran from Tashlin, skipping the many instances of nose-mockery.

At the end, Babiola said unbelieving, "Her kingdom for a kiss?"

"Yes, all she wanted was a kiss. But I couldn't."

Babiola smiled and pressed, "Was she too old and withered for your young lips?"

"No. I simply could not."

Septimius paused.

Babiola stared.

"My nose was too large for the situation, Babiola. It got in the way."

Babiola looked at her friend now like one who saw for the first time. She noted the ungainly nostrils and lifted a paw to her own flat face.

Septimius looked away.

Feeling the need to meet his disclosure with one of her own, Babiola leaned in and confided, "I am not a monkey, Septimius."

Septimius looked again at Babiola. And, though it was a monkey that sat before him, he knew what he was hearing was true.

"I am not a monkey," Babiola repeated, "and the queen who wanted a kiss from you is my mother."

Septimius's eyes widened.

Babiola continued, "I cannot fathom all that passed between you and the queen. I have no memory of Tiree and have no idea how and why I was born this way. But at least—and at last—I no longer mind my physique. Being a monkey let me save you."

She paused for Septimius to answer but he had yet to find one.

"It suited the kingdom of Tenpetal to make me a pet, a tradable source of amusement. Is that somehow worse than the kingdom of Tiree regarding me as disposable? All I want to know is, would you know me, my royal friend, from the other animals if I do not adorn myself? Will you know me if I cease to speak? Is my soul within my eyes, like I see the soul of a prince in yours?"

Septimius answered none of Babiola's questions. He had

ceased to hear the moment she revealed that Queen Valencia was her mother.

"Queen Valencia made *me* her heir," he said. "But Tiree is *your* kingdom, Babiola. Tiree's throne belongs to you." The prince stood up all at once, but sat quickly back down. The boat rocked violently in response to his passion, but he continued his speech like a priest behind a pulpit, "It is your land. You are heir. You shall at least rule *with* me!"

Babiola smiled a crooked smile. "It is impossible. To all but you, I am at best a trained monkey. But If I am seen, *really* seen by you, I am satisfied."

The prince opened his mouth to argue, but Babiola shook her head and went on, "Happenstance was supposed to kill me, but tossed me out. Why would I return to where I am not wanted? Being alive is victory enough."

Prince Septimius understood very little, but more than ever before.

It was Babiola's turn to sermonize. "The most important piece of information Happenstance provided while I was under her roof concerns neither of us, dear Prince. I don't know how she knows all she knows, but I have no reason to doubt her witchy words. The pirates who wanted me have taken Finita instead. I must make this right, even if it means taking her place."

The prince sat still and silent. Babiola wondered and waited. When at last he answered, it was with grave decisive authority, "First, we go home."

I wonder where my home is, thought the passenger-monkey to herself, and how we will accomplish a home-going with no sail.

But she did not trouble the captain-prince for details.

Somewhere on the northbound journey, the Crown Prince of Tenpetal grew faint once again from his wounds. The fresh water ran dry and his stomach began to ache. He and his little monkey curled up together in the bottom of *Morning Star* and passed into oblivion. Neither noticed the ship looming in the distance. Neither sat up and saw the *Quimpus* until their little vessel was lifted from the waves and hauled upon the deck of the great three-masted mother ship.

Babiola and Septimius had no energy for words when Queen Valencia ordered them to comfortable quarters. Babiola might have found her voice if she had known how close the queen had come to having her throat slit. But all who stood on deck saw that beyond all doubt, the monkey belonged to the heir-apparent of Tiree, and that, in some way, the animal had saved him.

[17]

THE CAPRICIOUSNESS OF MOTHERHOOD

There's an empty hollow afterward
From being used and using
With little loves come little lies
Excuses and excusing

The first thing Septimius noted upon returning to his home island of Tenpetal was Babiola's silence. She had said very little aboard the great ship but would at least make light conversation in the privacy of their cabin. Now she spoke not a word.

The first thing Queen Valencia noted upon arriving at the island of Tenpetal was that there were monkeys. She had grown used to their absence, having stripped their distastefulness from every tree of Tiree. Here on Tenpetal, there seemed to be the shape of one species or another perched on every other branch. No one but Babiola noted Valencia's subtle recoil every time the cry of a puchin or the screech of the mosmaret rang out from the surrounding forest.

As the landing party approached the palace. Babiola

became restless and refused to leave the arms of her friend, but even though he did his best to pet and calm her, she found no respite. News of the prince's miraculous return was cried house to house with ever-growing waves of excitement. With every jubilant cry of welcome, Septimius regained an old familiar confidence. But Babiola did not share his sense of safe return. She hid behind ever-thickening walls of wordlessness.

Both prince and monkey were relieved and surprised to look over the undulating crowd and see the friendly face of Quarta. The fourth Princess of Tenpetal had taken up residence in a neighborhood halfway between pier and palace. She stood observing the commotion from a wide porch. Without word, Babiola sprang from the arms of the much-heralded Crown Prince and into the arms of his much-surprised sister.

"My brother and Babiola too!" laughed Quarta. "I'm not sure which gives me more pleasure."

Septimius smiled wide and called back from the crowd, "It seems our monkey friend wants to end her journey here with you!"

"She can stay!" said Quarta. "I understand her desire to withdraw. But you must go on, lest you bring to my front door the rabble she and I wish to avoid."

"Keep your eye on her, Quarta. She is my friend," said Septimius, his voice barely heard above the fray.

Quarta was puzzled by little brother's solemn tone, but blew a kiss to assure him of her intention to keep faith.

THE MONKEY NOW GONE, Queen Valencia took Septimius's arm for the remainder of the upward stroll. "You must reintroduce me to your mother," she insisted. "We have not seen each other since childhood." With a giggle reminiscent of her very recent childishness she added, "I hope your mother does not mind my affectionate attachment to you."

"Mother will be pleased to be reacquainted, I'm sure," said Septimius with forced affect, missing Babiola's silent company all the more.

The reunion of mother and son was not dignified. Queen Maureen jettisoned both regality and privacy and ran down the cobblestones to take her long-lost son into her arms. She wept on and on like a child, pausing only to question what had happened to his beautiful nose. She kissed its brokenness and spoke to its bruises with great affection.

Queen Valencia stepped back, giving outward courtesy for the mother and child reunion. Inwardly she was appalled by the public petting of a full-grown man. Only by a hair did she stifle the laugh that crept up in her throat in response to the blind mother-love for the ridiculous nose. Valencia had but one loss to compare—a casualty she considered a stillbirth. She could not take in what it must be like for a fellow queen to receive a child back from the dead.

Queen Valencia flourished a bow and cleared her throat. Septimius, tired of the fuss, turned to answer her summons.

With grand formality the Crown Prince of Tenpetal and Heir-Apparent to Tiree reacquainted two sovereigns. Neither woman, in truth, remembered meeting before, but both greeted each other with affection. Maureen thanked Valencia effusively and gave her singular credit for the return of the beloved Crown Prince, assuring her of the finest suite and most magnificent celebration the kingdom of Tenpetal had to offer.

After dinner, and once the travelers had taken time to rest and wash and regain their land legs, a royal company assembled in rooms once occupied by the Dread Pirate Pelagio. Something about the suite still smelled of buccaneer, though no one who noticed breathed a complaint.

"I cannot thank you enough, dearest Valencia," Queen Maureen was saying once again, "for the return of the kingdom's beloved son."

"'Twas but a lucky intersection upon the sea, dearest Maureen. Both the prince and I wanted to return to Tenpetal, and here we are. The *Quimpus* always did make great speed. I do hope the *Morning Star* can be repaired. For all her smallness, she seems to bring our prince much joy."

At the mention of the *Morning Star,* King Egbert excused himself, saying he was needed at the docks. Prince Septimius desired to follow, but knew it would be some time before the ladies present would tolerate the exiting of another royal male. He congratulated his father silently on the astute maneuver.

"We have had so many losses, dear friend," Maureen said between sips of wine. "It is so nice, for once, to have fortune shine on us."

"Oh Sister Queen," answered Valencia, making up the phrase of familiarity on the spot, "tell me all. I wish to sympathize with your maternal heart."

Queen Maureen found Queen Valencia's wording rather odd, but never could resist an opportunity to speak of her children. "We have seven you know," she began with a tone familiar to Septimius. "In fact, my six princesses have names that form a poem ...[1] Septimius, whom you have returned to me, was given the middle name 'Gilbert.' A fact he tries to ignore."

"All of them grown? How are they situated now?" Queen Valencia asked, trying to gain a sense of the relational landscape. She felt Septimius slipping away—all attachment to her weakening with every passing minute he was home.

"Well my two lovely eldest girls, Prima and Secunda," said Maureen, "made fine matches. I fancy they are competing in childbearing, for each spring I must embark on a tour of the grandchildren—after pirate season of course—just to count heads."

Valencia laughed politely and Maureen continued, "Tertia entered a monastery, though neither I nor her father encouraged that path. Now Quinta packs her things to follow. Imagine! Two of my daughters spending their days offering up prayers. Can't hurt, I say. Can't hurt. We'll take all the help we can get from every quarter."

Valencia smiled in a way to communicate her utmost interest. Maureen took this as an invitation. "Quarta lives locally. She comes to have tea with me every Wednesday. The other days it is needlepoint, oil paints, and books, books, books." At this last piece of information, Valencia could smile with real sincerity. Her silent candor inspired Maureen to make a reciprocal inquiry of her own. "The news of King Hubert's death came much too late for me to send proper regards. Please know we sorrow with you. You have children to care for you, I presume?"

"I had a baby once ... " sighed Queen Valencia.

"Oh really, just one?"

"You would not understand in spite of your tender kindness, I fear. Her birth ... my pregnancy ... involved fairies. And I do not want to bother you with trifles. Many do not believe and I cannot say that I blame them. It sounds like nonsense to speak of it in spite of my sorrowful experience."

"Fairies! Really! Me too!" responded Maureen with unbridled delight. She crossed the floor and sat next to her guest, as if the two women were bosom friends. "So many girls! I so longed for a boy. The fairies can be helpful when they want to be."

Queen Valencia's thoughts pounded. Her emotions

exploded. How is it this woman was granted a seventh! For a change in gender! While she was robbed after a brief moment with one!

After a long silence, Valencia found a reply. "Yes ... fairies are helpful ... if they want to be. I must confess, though, I have been left injured by their unfairness and caprice."

Maureen took Valencia's hand in her own and murmured, "Oh Sister Queen, I understand loss. Do not think I have come thus far unscathed. From this very room in fact, I lost my dear Finita. The pirates wanted the monkey and the obstinate creature refused and ran. In revenge, cursed Pelagio took my precious Finita, and now we hear nothing but rumors."

Valencia took away her hand. She stood and paced, her face turning red in fury. All courtly decorum melted away as she voiced question upon burning question, "What in the world did the pirates want with a flea-bitten monkey? What made them come all this way for a palace pet? Demanding a princess I can understand but ... "

"Well, she did play the harpsichord," interjected Septimius, surprised at the passion on display.

"And speak French," added his mother in an attempt to regain some sense of seemliness.

"She t ... t ... talked?" stammered Valencia.

"Dear Septimius," cooed Maureen, "tell the story. Tell our dear guest how you got the monkey, how she was laid in your arms by an angel."

"Well not exactly an angel, mother," said Septimius, trying to discern the explosive state of affairs. "More like a footman. Out by the great Pier of King Pibrac on Tiree, you are familiar with it, Queen Valencia. I often sailed round your beautiful island but never came on shore to have the pleasure of meeting Your Majesty. The monkey, just a baby at the time, was dropped into my lap ... like the young man had intended to drop her into the sea and the *Morning Star* and I got in the way."

"She speaks ... She speaks ... " was all that Queen Valencia could say in response.

"And recites sonnets," said Queen Maureen.

"And is the truest friend a man could want," said Septimius. "So true I often forget she is a monkey."

"May I speak with you alone, Sister Queen?" asked Valencia, a tear streaming down her left cheek. "Queen to Queen. Mother to Mother."

THE ROOMS WERE CLEARED and not a soul could suspect what was about to come forth. Not a soul, that is, but Septimius. For a fleeting moment, he was tempted to stand outside and press his ear against the closed door. But, deciding that some knowledge did not belong even to a Crown Prince, he slipped instead into the night air and made his way down the wide lane to Quarta's quarters.

Behind closed doors, for the first time in her life Queen Valencia of Tiree confessed her sins. In heartfelt angst, she told all she had done. How she had begged for a child, given birth, but had in the end refused to mother.

For the first time in *her* life, Queen Maureen of Tenpetal was speechless. She listened and nodded and wept a little herself. Some tears were for her Sister Queen. Some were of regret. She had treated Babiola—a princess—well below the honor due her rank. Weeks later this beautiful shame was impermeably coated over with the shellac of "how could I have known." But in that moment, Queen Maureen sat in solidarity with another weeping woman, treating her as an equal.

Solidarity between two women of high station bred to

compete, wired to envy, and honed to undercut is a magic that cannot be resisted, however fleeting it might have been. It is a magic that can force feuding fairies into odd acts of collusion.

For the first time in nearly two centuries, Fairy Sabellia and Fairy Marcionna appeared together in the same room, looking shocked and almost contrite. Sabellia had been at the north pole up to her elbows in an experiment involving a giant teakettle and the three mystical states of water.[2] Marcionna had been in her mentor's basement, researching the practicality of harnessing the bipolar mood swings of a fabled wind goddess. Neither had wished to be interrupted, but a deeper law, more profound than any laid down by magician's guild protocol, had summoned the fairies against their wishes.

A QUEENLY BOND AND FAIRY FEUD

Of all ideals we hail as good
No higher honor than motherhood
A man, his soul might self-destroy
But still remain a mama's boy
A man looks to mother,
despite a good wife
And a daughter's her mother
by the end of her life

Sabellia stood at attention in the royal suite, this time at full height and without her broom. Marcionna stood beside her looking less than pleased. Upon Marcionna's open palm sat a curious glass container, shining in a color halfway between ruby red and sky blue. Before either fairy could say a word, Sabellia snatched the bottle from her sister fairy and hid it deep within the folds of her robe.

Like two actresses continuing a play after a long intermission, and with no more than a sideways glance to each other in acknowledgment, the fairies staged a performance like no other. Both bowed as one like seasoned thespians to the audience of monarchs. Each took up recitations of a script springing from the innermost thoughts of the queens. With frightening accuracy, the private monologue of the matriarchs was spoken aloud by the fairies.

Sabellia gave voice to Valencia, perfecting her delivery down to the very wavelength of inflection (S as V). Marcionna became Maureen, honing her voice to capture every nuance of tonality (M as M). The lines and stage direction were as follows—

[Both cast members face and address the audience.]

SaV: "A pox on the hobgoblin that turned my beautiful daughter into a monkey!"

MaM: "A hex on the pixie that gave my son a monstrous nose."

[Cast faces each other, hands on hips. MaM stage right / SaV stage left.]

MaM [right finger wagging]: "You think a fairy destroyed your chances at motherhood? Those chances were ruined by your bored purposelessness long before Babiola's hairy birth. Self-amusement is no reason to be granted a child to raise."

SaV [left finger wagging]: "And who are you, you sagging belly of unbridled fertility! Having seven brats is no proud resume. Motherhood for you has been the imprinting of your own sorry sins upon six miniatures, plus one."

MaM: "Where is your monkey now? Did you have her strangled in her sleep or drowned?"

SaV: "You think yourself better than I? What is your youngest daughter now? A pirate's whore!"

MaM: "Fool! Do you think that having babies cures a woman's inner wounds? We birth them, teach them, protect them, and then they leave us to old age. I have suffered more loss than you can begin to fathom."

Both fairies now turned again towards the audience to gauge the effect of their savage performance.

The two sat in silence, mouths agape.

Each fairy scanned each queen, hopeful for any signs of emotional fissure or relational crack.

Sabellia sighed. Marcionna moaned.

The sister-bond remained unbroken. In fact, each woman had wrapped arms round the other to support against the torrent of shocking truth and errorless insult. Not an arrow had been deflected. All pierced through, each to each, pain for pain.

According to the Oracles of Chasmic Magic, one minute of theater was all the time allowed to negate the sorcery that had called forth the fairies. It had been a desperate act to defy a calling to account for the damage done by each. The theatrical act had failed and the fairies, though they would never confess it outright, were bound to serve the wishes of the queens— one per monarch. Neither could have predicted the bond between the queens would hold under direct onslaught. Neither would have thought their assertive cooperation would have been defeated by the strange passive unity between royalty barely reacquainted.

Sabellia approached Queen Valencia and bowed. With curled lip she spat out a last desperate accusation, "What grew inside you, mother of a monkey, was a reflection of yourself. If you had loved the little girl with a modicum of the selflessness required of every mother, she would have transformed alongside you, both of you becoming more human. But you thought only of yourself and sent her away to her doom."

Queen Valencia sensed the stakes were high, but also felt the fairy hesitate. She countered with vehemence, "You changed my baby into a monkey! Do not place this at my feet. I am no more fallen than any other woman."

"Spells on babies is what wicked fairies do … "

"Undo it."

"I suppose I must, your majesty. This round you are victorious, much to my surprise. But the matter is not as straightforward as you might wish. Besides, you smell of dwarf magic. You've had work done, haven't you."

"Done and undone," said Valencia.

"What about me?" piped Maureen.

"You are my problem, I'm afraid," said Marcionna with a sigh.

"I want my little girl back! Unsullied and innocent."

"Your case is beyond complicated, my queen," answered Marcionna. "It is knotted through and through. I may have had a hand in the birth of your son, but you produced Sexta Finita with no help from me. She chose the role of pirate princess quite willingly. I'm not sure what power, if any, I hold."

Maureen cast about but found no argument. Still, she sensed Marcionna's incertitude. "I believe the simple fact that you are here means I profit in some way … "

Both queens stood together, arm in arm, staring down their foes.

"We want our daughters back," their majesties insisted in chorus.

"Do they *want* to return?" came back the fairies' synchronized answer, turning in unison to face them.

The queens fell silent.

Sabellia's eyes glazed over, and droning verse came from her barely parted lips—

> *Finita approaches on the wave*
> *Babiola sits within the town*

Do either wish for mother-dear
Or does the love flow one way round?

"What she's saying," said Marcionna, cutting through the chanting obfuscation, "is that we have magic to offer, but the girls have got to do their part. Mother-daughter relations are a tangled weave. All wills must synchronize or all purple dust and magic rhymes are mute. Not even fourth-level druids ... "

"Enough rambling," interrupted Sabellia, producing the hidden bottle from beneath the folds in her robe. She placed it upon a table saying, "Daughters and mothers must be present and fully engaged. Both must breathe in the dust together. But what the puff of purple hawthorn powder produces depends upon a daughter's walk and a mother's eye."

"Mother's eye?" said Valencia.

"Be careful how you see her," instructed Marcionna.

"Daughter's walk?" said Maureen.

"No sense telling you about something you'll just want to control," returned Sabellia with caustic bitterness. "But mind you—how you see them is how *you'll* be."

And with these cryptic instructions, Marcionna and Sabellia saluted and parted from the queens of Tiree and Tenpetal, exiting in a manner only women who perfectly hate each other can.

THAT SAME HOUR, Septimius entered the humble home of his sister and found Babiola eating beside Quarta's hearth. He watched Babiola's restful quietness from the entrance. Babiola did not turn as Quarta approached her brother and offered a warm kiss on a cheek chilled by the night air.

"Has she told you much?" asked Septimius.

Quarta shook her head. "She speaks only when spoken to."

She's using language less and less, thought Septimius to himself. The monkey's increasing silence worried him.

Septimius took a seat next to his friend by the fire, "I think you should come with me to the palace, Babiola."

Babiola looked up, monkey eyebrows raised in incredulity.

"Do they want for entertainment?"

"No ... It's your mother. I think it would do her good to see you."

"She saw me on the ship," Babiola answered and turned once more to watch the flames.

"Things have changed, and much is changing still ... I think you have a part to play."

"No. I will stay here. I have no desire to perform ever again in Tenpetal or any other palace."

"What is asked of you is not ... cannot be playacting. Unexpected guests have arrived. Your mother is weeping. It is all very strange."

"If I go, I will only regress further. They treat me like an animal, so an animal is what I'll be."

"You are not a monkey to me, Babiola."

Babiola wiped away a tear and Septimius wiped away one of his own.

"She cast me off as a newborn, Septimius, and spoke not a word to me aboard the *Quimpus*."

Septimius did not argue. "There's a change afoot. If she is not calling for you this very hour, she will be soon."

Septimius stood and took Babiola by the hand. She rose and allowed herself to be led out through the open front door.

"What is this woman to me?" the princess-monkey asked with flattened tone.

"One who, just perhaps, deserves our tears."

"Whatever do you mean?" Babiola asked, coming to a standstill upon the cobblestone.

Septimius pulled at his chin then pulled at her hand.

The two continued onward with Septimius's thoughts rattling around looking for the right words.

"My mother's pride made me blind to the very nose on my face," he said finally. "I embraced that blindness, loved it until I made it my own. We are all connected, strength and weakness, but especially parent and child."

Babiola did not answer but neither did she hang back or slacken the pace.

WHEN BABIOLA ENTERED the room where her mother stood, there was no noticeable difference between her and any monkey in any tree of Tenpetal, unless one looked into her eyes. Valencia did not gaze into her daughter's face and, for her part, Babiola did not offer it.

Queen Valencia saw only a monkey.

So a monkey is what Queen Valencia became.

Upon breathing hawthorn powder rising up from shattered glass, Queen Valencia of Tiree had her daughter back—nose for nose, paw for paw, tail for tail.

A mother-monkey's cry rang out and Babiola was cut to the heart. She saw her part in the madness, her hardness, her refusal to grieve. With a monkey cry she responded in turn and flew to her mother's arms where a bitter happiness enveloped them both.

[19]

MOONLIGHT SAIL AND STOWAWAY

Old lady—young lady—old lady—monkey
What might you next time transform to?
What shape's best for you to love me?
Who's the mother I was born to?

For three days and three nights, mother and daughter monkeys were absorbed in a wordless reunion, neither taking notice of any human company. Valencia's eyes contained something soulful and hard-to-name, but otherwise she was an animal without speech. Babiola, muted by sorrow and solidarity, spoke no longer.

While Septimius wandered the halls feeling lost, Maureen sat and wept. Her tears were the bewildered expression of one left behind and forgotten. She shuddered at the fate of her sister-queen all the while yearning for her youngest girl more and more.

In between sniffles, Queen Maureen hunted down the dusty remains of purple hawthorn. The shards of glass had been swept away by dutiful staff. But, by scraping grout in secret, and combing every thread of the woolen rug, she gathered almost a teaspoon of the magic dust and hid it away in a silken handkerchief. Who knows? she thought. My turn with Finita may come ... who knows?

In his second night restlessly haunting the palace corridors, Septimius found his father's study door closed. Secrets were out of character with King Egbert. So was the alarming tone emanating from within. This time the prince did not resist pressing ear to oak to hear more.

"The *Landeven*, are you sure?"

"Quite sure, your majesty."

"Pirates in the mouth of *my* harbor?! They dare come so close?"

"I believe, sire, the enemy thinks you will not use the castle cannon, considering who is on board."

Septimius could not discern his father's next words, but he could feel, even through solid wood, the rising intensity. King Egbert raised his volume and a single word sliced through —"Fire."

"But sir, the princess."

"Did I stutter?! Fire the cannon. She has long been dead to us."

There was a silence.

"At first light of dawn," said the king, "Pack all cannon tight: powder, shrapnel, and ball. Have trusted men stand by. I am through being played. I am done with domesticated predictability."

"Yes sir."

The servant, exiting, saluted the Crown Prince in the shadows, but did not pause.

Septimius heard his father continue on, addressing now the empty room, "I should have restored my manhood long ago, long before they dared to lay their hands upon a child of Tenpetal."

Septimius's head pounded as he made his way to his quarters. So his father preferred to sink the *Landeven* than bear more shame. Speaking to the king would do no good. Septimius knew the tone. His only hope was stealth, and the freedom that belonged to a crown prince.

Septimius went to his room to rest and eat. It was only the first watch and there was time. Though he ate until he was full, not a wink of sleep would come. Frustrated, he rose and dressed—black shirt and trousers, black scabbard and spy glass. He wondered how far along were the repairs to the *Morning Star*. She needed to be seaworthy at least in part. The trip would be short and he was determined to board no other.

Halfway to her place of docking, Septimius spun round for someone followed. Left, right, down—no one. He continued on, but again a rustling met his ears. Looking up, he saw a familiar face with wide, glowing eyes reflecting the night sky. Babiola smiled, dropped to the ground, and took his hand.

"Why do you come?" asked Septimius, wanting to hear her voice more than he cared to know her reasons.

"I have monkey ears and know what you are about," said Babiola.

Septimius's heart soared in the darkness, lifted by that single sentence.

"What of your mother?" said the prince. "You two have a lifetime to make up for and three days is hardly enough."

"There is much to bear and overcome," answered Babiola softly. "She is a monkey, a soulful monkey, but an animal all the same. If only I had entered more ladylike, she might have seen the truer me ... and become her truer self."

"Go back," commanded the prince, not letting go of her hand.

Babiola kept pace.

"I am helpless to repent past my blind self-sorrowing," she confessed. "I doubt more tears of remorse would do my mother any good."

Babiola's tone was so soaked in regret that Septimius's pace slowed to a crawl. He felt a great weight tug his heart, anchored in her deeps. He would order her back, he would call the guard.

Babiola spoke again, pushing back the heaviness with a touch of levity, "I cannot speak monkey, even being one, so it seems I am of no further use to my mother the queen. But I do know something of helping royals escape."

"That you do," Septimius smiled before adding with a shudder, "I would be starving in despair, still locked in the Tashlin prison hut, waiting for a beating."

Babiola squared her little shoulders like a soldier and went on, "Friend Prince, the fate of Finita is my burden, not yours. It is my fault she was taken captive—my overblown, idiotic fame. I, the highly-sought-after magic monkey, caused pirates to invade your peaceful home. Let my monkey eyes and monkey ears and nimble monkey hands undo what might still be undone."

Septimius shook his head. "No, friend, if I had taken her on a single adventure, she would not have had to find her own. Her undoing is my doing. Still, I am glad to have you with me."

So content were Babiola and Septimius in each other's company that neither heard the rustling of a second follower not many paces behind.

IT TOOK some doing to retrieve the *Morning Star*. She was up on scaffolding to have her bottom scraped and painted. New sails and ensign were folded neatly nearby. Septimius was glad for Babiola's deft fingers and silent companionship. Her nimble agility cut the labor by more than half. Still, the work to set sail took hours, and both were glad no alarm sounded or dock man approached.

Dock workers took little notice of the prince for they were used to him coming and going at all hours. All still awake stared out towards the mouth of the harbor where the *Landeven* sat silhouetted in the moonlight, glowing eerily above the water-line. All the while, rumors swirled in every quarter that the cannons were being refitted.

AFTER SETTING SAIL, Septimius laid out the possibilities, "I was thinking you could scout about, Babiola. No problem for you to climb straight up the side and then come back to tell me who's awake, if there is a watchman, and if he's sober."

Babiola smiled and nodded, but said not a word.

"I wonder," said Septimius softly, "if sister really is housed in the captain's quarters. Surely not ... "

Stealth and wordless understanding cloaked the *Morning Star*. Whole constellations twinkled above as the little ship drew close to the side of the larger vessel, anchored and asleep. It would have been a beautiful night for a sail if not for the perilousness of their mission.

Septimius looked to his friend. No face looked back. He scanned the hulking side of the *Landeven*, but saw no monkey form beginning the ascent. He stared overboard for bobbing head or tail. The sea was glass.

A voice called from above, high on *Morning Star's* newly

repaired mast. A monkey shriek pierced the night and every soul within a half mile. The howl morphed slowly into speech as Babiola, famed monkey of the Rogasian Archipelago, called to the enemies of the House of Tenpetal in perfect English, with the allure of a siren.

[20]

CHEEKS WET WITH TEARS COME LIGHT OF DAY

I'm dying to see you Nestorio!
Come greet your eager monkey belle!
I want to taste your sweetest fruits
I want to please you more than well
My speech and music, do not forget
Forgive my shyness when last we met

In horror, Septimius saw lanterns lit one by one aboard the *Landeven*. The vessel grew brighter and brighter with each line of Babiola's recitation. One small flame at time, the hulking pirate ship began to compete with the luminosity of the moon.

"What is this!?" came the booming voice of Nestorio himself. "Who wakes the captain and why!?"

His hot words carried anger, but even Septimius could see the pirate's eyes were shining, a man drunk with anticipation of a prize.

"Parlay!" returned Babiola at the top of her lungs. "I come to trade. Last time a dread pirate set foot on Tenpetal, he came for a world-renowned monkey and nabbed an adolescent girl.

Give this princeling his sister and you shall have me—Babiola! The talking, harpsichord playing, yodeling, bilingual monkey! Music to draw thousands! Sonnets in impeccable French!"

Nestorio rubbed his palms and shook his head in disbelief.

Babiola surveyed the captain and the gathering crew stumbling on deck. She said, "Captain Nestorio, I stagnate on this backwater island, wasting away. This inbred family of royal fools treats me as a palace mascot. I hope you have not forgotten your promise of a world tour."

"Why no, magnificent monkey," called back Nestorio, "my offer still stands. But why do you come to me in the dark of night? Why do I hear urgency in your voice? Why break into my sleep? Can't we come to generous terms over a generous breakfast?"

"We must come to an understanding at once, sir, for you have overplayed your hand. Finita is valuable only to one—the princeling standing below me in a leaky excuse for a rowboat. This last-born boy wants his big sissy back—what's left of her. Her father the king, however, will put cannonballs through *Landeven's* starboard flank at first light."

Babiola paused for dramatic effect, then added, "How am I to sail away to glory on a sunken pirate ship?"

The threat of destructive violence brought immediate enlightenment to the mind of the pirate captain.

"You, dearest monkey, for Finita? Consider it done! Let me go gather the wench and what few belongings she clings to."

The wench was already on deck, standing two paces behind.

Absorbing every word.

A second shriek split the night, "Me? For a monkey!?"

Nestorio jumped and turned, yet was quick to make answer, "Yes! You wandering trifle! You who thinks no man's attention too low for you. You constant distraction to my entire crew. Go where you are still somehow wanted. Your time upon my decks has ended."

Babiola's eyes widened, but she cloaked her sad shock and crouched to spring from the mast of *Morningstar* to the rail of *Landeven*. She had come to be traded and had heard nothing to change her mind.

Septimius sat bewildered. Gone was sweet Finita and all her adventuring innocence. The stoic accuracy of his father's discernment seared like salt water seeping into a thousand cuts.

A SKIRMISH aboard the *Landeven* began. Sexta Finita was not eager to go home with little brother. Nestorio was eager to be rid of a onetime novelty, and zealous to gain what had once slipped through his hands.

A skirmish aboard the *Morning Star* also began. Babiola, mid-jump, found her left leg snagged in an ever-tightening noose. Emerging from under the bow seat, a second, older monkey with bright intelligent eyes tethered the younger. And without pause, Valencia leapt to climb aboard the *Landeven* in her daughter's place.

Septimius clung to the sides of the *Morning Star* as she rocked while Babiola lay stunned in the cradle of the hull. The leap of Valencia had pushed the little boat to double her former distance from the pirate vessel. As *Morning Star* continued to drift away, Septimius watched the bizarre story unfold.

No one aboard the *Landeven* noticed the substitution. A monkey was a monkey was a monkey, unless you took the time to look into her eyes—a habit not known to pirates. The moon, as if in cahoots, shrouded herself behind a cumulus cloud. In the ruckus, Nestorio did not perceive when his kerchief was stripped from his neck to form a makeshift skirt.

Valencia began to dance.

The sailors began to clap and sing.

Sexta Finita continued to screech.

With a wave of a hand, Nestorio ordered the anchor hauled up and sails raised.

"I'll bring your princess back to you," he called out with a laugh triumphant, "when she is more eager to come home!"

Septimius looked down to Babiola and up again to the pirate ship. "He thinks he has *you*. Do not move!"

Babiola obeyed, mostly. She mouthed the word "mother" once and shivered, laboring to catch her breath.

EVEN AS THE separation between the two ships grew, the drama aboard *Landeven* rode upon the waves, continuing towards its climax. Another voice and figure took center stage on the deck headed out to sea. The form of an older woman displaced the monkey. From this commanding physique issued forth the voice of a queen.

Sober eyes were few aboard the *Landeven,* but all was crisp and clear and unmistakable to the audience upon *Morning Star.* Septimius's eyes were dry with staring. Babiola, now sitting up, took in the specter like a prophet caught up in mystic visions. Magic was unwinding before all who had eyes to see it.

The voice of Sexta, still mocking, shifted in its tone, "She's an old woman! Senile and shriveled! You've been had, Captain! A changeling! Your little monkey escapes back to shore and you must run up all sails and flee before my father's guns!"

Finita was cackling now. "Dread, O Nestorius, King Egbert of Tenpetal, or go down to your watery grave!"

The last thing the spectators on *Morning Star* heard, as *Landeven* sailed out of reach of canon, was the commanding voice of Queen Valencia, "You will take me at once to my flag-ship *Quimbus.*"

By the turn of the tiller, Septimius could tell the pirate captain had obeyed. "Of all things beyond prediction ... " he murmured.

Still staring out after the *Landeven,* the prince took Babiola by the hand. "I believe Dread Pirate Nestorio is being moth-ered ... and he does not seem to mind."

"I suppose, like many, he yearns for his own," was Babiola's soft answer.

By her tone, Septimius knew that magic was at work, even upon his own vessel. He turned just in time to see the last unweaving of the purple hawthorn's spell—wondrous to behold. The Babiola whose fingers laced with his was now a human girl. Draped in Tenpetal's royal green banner, she sat staring out at the rising sun, young and lovely. Her hair, dark as the fur on a speehider monkey, billowed in the morning breeze. Her eyes matched the purple trim of the rippling cloth clinging to her slender frame.

Septimius would have fallen overboard, like one struck by a bolt of shock, except for the creeping self-consciousness concerning his nose. His entrancement with the beautiful wonder before him was quelled by a silent apology for what he offered in return.

"How are you here ... like this ... and with me?"

As the tide continued to push the *Morning Star* towards shore, Babiola took Septimius's other hand and faced him. The rhyming lies she had told less than an hour before were eclipsed now by the true—

> *When mother-daughter minds are one*
> *And leaping sacrifice to save*
> *Is made above the harbor waves*

All illusions come undone

"Where did you learn that?"

"It is one of the many palace sonnets a trained monkey is forced to memorize," Babiola said. "It seems there is more to Tenpetal poetry than I was capable of believing."

"How is it I never heard that poem before?" asked the prince.

"It is usually recited in French," winked the princess.

"Ah yes, French. I never bothered to learn."

Septimius went quiet. His friend's lovely transformation was accounted for, at least as far as magic can be. Still, he grappled with his own glaring flaw. He raised his hands to cover his face. But before the fingers of Septimius, Crown Prince of the Tenpetal Islands, could cover his ridiculously large nose, Babiola, Princess of Tiree, touched it with her human lips.

And with each kiss, it shrank a little.

Babiola did not stop her kisses until tears ran down both their cheeks.

NOTES

1. UNEXPECTED GUESTS

1. *Walter and the Raven*, first edition
2. Hilda was fourteen but, being slight in form and late to bloom, did not look a day past ten.

4. TOBIT AND PASHA

1. *In Light of the New Moon*, third edition

1. A WISH TO BE MORE WIDELY READ

1. Whether he would not, or could not, none knew.

3. SEVENTH-BORN WITH STATELY NOSE

1. Nursemaids were never used in the kingdom of Tenpetal though diaper-maids were kept on retainer.
2. Queen Maureen took comfort when even the king, in everyday usage, also fell to calling the girl by her middle name—a word that did not remind His Majesty of an activity of which his wife had grown tired.

5. CRASHING CHANGE AND PIRATE LUST

1. Rumor had it that the queen of the region had gone mad, and in her ravings she could not bear the sight or sound of monkeys large or small, far or near.

9. DREAMS OF YOUTH AND MAGIC CHALK

1. Mr. Bunkle was having a flashback to the folly of a forefather, Rumpelstilt-skin—a dwarf who wove his true name into his bargaining. Rumple's Folly is the short form for a much longer, somewhat crass dwarfian proverb.

2. An ancient rendition of an extended version of the poem at the opening of this chapter.

10. BETTER SONGS THAN IDLE TALK

1. This chapter is rather short so if the reader would like to sing full force as well, below are the lyrics uninterrupted. Feel free to sing it though several times to fill in the usual time allotted for a reading—
   Should I set sail for a beach on Tiree? O!
   What care I of Tiree?
   I have never set foot on its shore, O
   But I find myself aching for more, O
   Where you sail makes no difference to me
   Chorus:
   Hey-dee dee,
   Mis-er-able me,
   Wide and long is the sea
   I was loved by my mama as an itty bitty baby
   May I die in the arms of a wrinkled old lady
   Should I sail towards Thimbleweed, O!
   Wide and long is the sea
   Pirates there harden the soul, O
   I am soft in the middle you know, O
   Where you sail makes no difference to me.
   Chorus
   I come from Tenpetal shore, O!
   Your home has no hold on me
   Give a kiss to my mother
   Six sisters and no brother
   Where we sail makes no difference to me.
   Chorus

11. TAKE CARE THE COMPANY YOU KEEP

1. "What a pity" or "too bad" or, if one feels indifferent, "I could care less."

13. HUMAN HANDS AND MONKEY PAWS

1. Six princesses playing dress-up, year after year, had prepared her well.
2. A chapter break should go here but the author does not wish to throw off the rhymes in the table of contents. A similar state of affairs occurs in Chapter 13.

15. AT LAST PRINCE CHARMING BENDS TO KISS

1. Prufrock's *Walter and the Raven*, in the original Bohemian, is not exactly ordinary but to Mr. Bunkle—whose reading was wide, wild, and peculiar—it was child's play.
2. Straightforward disenchantments do not require the cooperation or permission of a Majesty. Re-enchantments are another matter altogether and are the domain of third generation arch-wizards.

17. THE CAPRICIOUSNESS OF MOTHERHOOD

1. Since all in the room but Valencia tuned out, you, dear reader, may as well. If you would like to read the recitation again, it is printed in chapter three. The rest of us will refocus our attention at the end when Queen Maureen was saying ...
2. Her work was heavily highlighted by one Thuria Von Mulligan, High Mistress of Watershed Palace, though Mistress Thuria found Sabellia's hypothesis questionable.